My Best Friend Tim

Marty Celaya

My Best Friend Tim
by Marty Celaya

Printed in the United States of America

ISBN 9781613790113

www.xulonpress.com

Forward

I'll never forget the first time I saw Marty Celaya. I was going to the local junior high dance at Parnell Park. This was a place where the future "John Travoltas" used to get together.

I was already a semi-legend at my school for my famous Soul Train moves. Upon entering the door, I was a little shocked at what I saw before me... a guy with similar moves that could definitely challenge everything I could bring to the floor.

If anyone could tell you some funny stories about me, it would definitely be Marty. Marty has been my friend, my wing-man, and even at times my prayer partner.

We've seen the highest places in life, and experienced some very difficult times together as well.

Reading Marty's stories for this book brought a smile to my face because in the midst of a very serious mission of helping people's lives, I was reminded once again that life is good.

Tim Storey

April, 2010

Dedication

I would like to dedicate this book to my wonderful children, Sara Celaya and Adam Celaya.

I have found out in life that the more I grow as a person, and the older I get, I tend to see life a little bit differently everyday. What I mean is that I am learning to appreciate the important things in life, and it's certainly the people in my life!

I thank God for giving us two of the most amazing, awesome children who are healthy, smart, intelligent, funny, good-looking, and especially, believers in Christ.

I believe that both of you will make huge positive impacts in this world as you go for your dreams keeping God at the center of your lives.

I have told you both since you were little, and I'll tell you again; You are champions, you're winners, and you're special.

Sara and Adam, I am so proud to have you as my children; you are truly the joy of Papa's life.

Love,

Dad

"There's a difference between a good idea and a God idea."

Tim Storey

Introduction

Over many wonderful years, I've had the very special privilege of knowing Tim Storey as a mentor, leader, brother, and close friend. From the age of twelve, my life has been enriched through my friendship with Tim, and I am truly a better person today because of him.

Tim Storey has had a huge impact upon my life in many positive ways. To have a friend like Tim over so many years is not only rare, it's been quite special. Tim led me to Christ when I was nineteen years old, and has helped me over the years to become a minister and an encourager to many people.

My entire family has and continues to be blessed through the friendship of Tim Storey. I will always be grateful to him.

As you journey though the next several pages, it's my hope that you catch a glimpse of Tim Storey perhaps in a different way than you may know him. Get to know the character, the funny guy, the man of wisdom, and the long-time friend through many short stories and real life experiences I've shared with Tim first hand.

Get ready to laugh, cry, learn, and laugh some more as I share my moments with "My Best Friend Tim."

Marty Celaya

"Enjoy the rhythm of life."

Tim Storey

Contents

**For Chapter Video Interviews with Tim and Marty, go to:
www.EncouragementIntl.org**

Chapter One

The Early Years, Jr. High and High School

Touchdown!

It was a sunny normal day in Southern California. Our Jr. High team, the Hillview Huskies, was ready to take on our cross-town rivals, the Granada Matadors, in the big football game of the year. We had all heard of the little dark kid from Granada who was supposed to be really fast and good at the game. I was playing on the junior varsity team on the south end of the field.

When our game ended (we got hammered, by the way), I walked over towards the varsity game to help cheer on our Huskies. I had not been there on the fifty yard line for more than a minute or two, when suddenly the quarterback for the Matadors dropped back in the pocket to throw long.

The next thing I saw was this skinny scrawny black kid with big hair come shooting out of the pack going deep. The quarterback unloaded what we call, "The Long Bomb."

My eyes followed the ball through the air right into the hands of little Timmy Storey. Touchdown! The crowd for the Matadors went crazy, while our team's supporters became a bit quiet. Believe it or not, the very first time I saw this guy, he was running downfield for the score.

Well, I can honestly say this would be the first of many more touchdowns in life for Tim; however, there have been real life fumbles and bruises along the way as well. What I'll always remember is my first view of Tim. A winner from day one!

Freshman Year - Cut From The Team.

After Jr. High in Whittier, California, most of the kids from my school went to either California High School or La Serna High School up in the hills. Because of where I lived, I was one of a small group of guys and girls who went to Monte Vista High School on the west side of town.

This is the school where Tim went as well. We started hanging around each other during the tryouts for the freshman basketball team.

Tim and I were totally confident that we would make the squad. (We both had a few years of street basketball under our belts.) What was interesting was that the coach had a unique way of picking his team.

We all lined up on the free-throw line, waiting anxiously as the coach gave us one more look-over. He looked for a guy who could perhaps rebound, but couldn't make a shot if his life depended on it; or a guy who could dribble the ball well, but could do nothing else. Our problem was that we were all-around players! Our second problem was that we *both* got cut from the team!

One by one, the coach chose his players, asking them to come and stand next to him. It was the feeling from elementary school when we would be on the playground, hoping to be picked on a winning team. After all of the players were chosen, Tim and I found ourselves standing in the group whose careers just ended.

That day, Tim and I walked home from school dejected, telling each other how stupid the coach was. We couldn't believe the audacity of this coach who bypassed our superstar talent! As we walked down Leffingwell Avenue, Tim's mom Bessie came driving up in the brown Pinto and said, "Get in." She drove us through the taco fast food place, and the next thing you knew, we were smiling again!

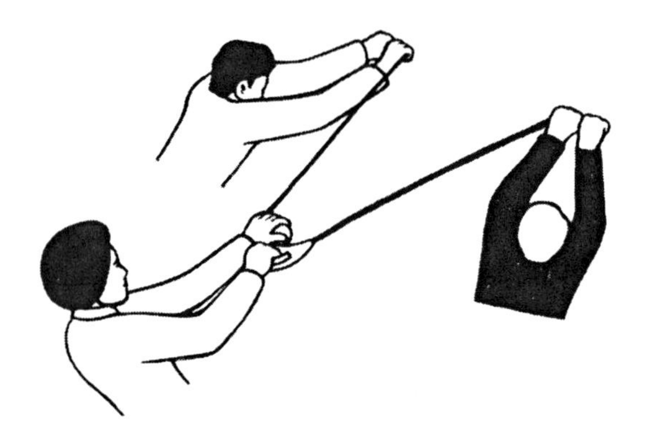

The Giant Sling Shot!

It was a Friday night party at Jaime Harris's big house on the other side of Creek Park. Mike, Larry, Mark, and I were just a few of the guys hanging out with Storey that night. We were a bit bored when Tim said, "Hey guys, let's create a giant sling shot and shoot water balloons over the trees into the party!" We're talking about a hundred yards away with a little creek in between - with several trees to go over.

Always the creative one, Tim came up with some surgical tubing - two pieces at least five feet in length – and tied them to each side of a towel. Tim said, "Two of you guys hold the surgical tubing and I'll launch the first one!" Tim set the water balloon in the towel, and began to pull, stretching the giant sling shot about fifteen feet back.

With everything he had, Tim launched the longest water balloon in the history of the world (up until that time, of course)! We all watched in amazement as it sailed past the creek, over the trees, and right into the crowd of people partying in the back yard of the Harris's house. Mike, Larry, Mark and I laughed hysterically during this high school military attack.

Immediately upon hearing the screams, Tim said, "Quick, give me another water balloon!" We bombed them good that night at the direction of our commander-in-chief, Tim Storey.

Stealing the Rabbits!

I'll never forget the night when we decided to steal the rabbits that were running through the yard of the little farm house by the school.

As we pulled up late at night in one of our friends' cars, Tim said, "Stop the car." The moonlight lit the way for what was about to happen next. He jumped out of the car, and - because he was the fastest runner out of all of us - he pounced on that poor little rabbit and actually caught it. One of us jumped out and somehow caught the second rabbit, but it was not easy.

The next thing you know we are stealing the cute little fury creatures with big ears in the Southern California moonlight driving away from the crime scene. As we were laughing out loud, we decided to do what any small group of high school buddies would do when you steal the rabbits. We drove to the home of one of the girls from our school and saw that her car door was unlocked. I seem to remember Tim putting the rabbits in the girl's car; I will not be held accountable.

The next morning at school, everyone was talking about how the rabbits ended up in the young lady's car! It was the talk of the lunch hour with everyone trying to solve the mystery. Well Laryn, the word is out; now you know who the culprits were.

Look! It's An Imposter!

Back in the day, there was a show on TV called Superstars. It was famous athletes who competed against other well-known athletes in different sports that they weren't skilled in. A football star would run a race on a track against a swimmer, or a golfer would do an obstacle course against a baseball star. You get the picture. Well, our senior year in high school, we decided to have the Superstar Competition at Monte Vista High.

It was a sunny day, and the crowd of students had assembled for this all-star competition. The fastest runner in the entire league was our friend, Mark Sponsler. I was paired up to run the 440 run against this super fast sprinter.

Mark got in lane one, while I staggered out in the last lane putting me out front at the start. With the crowd laughing and screaming, "Good luck Marty!" knowing I was moments away from being humiliated by our school's best athlete, the gun went off! I quickly began my turn around the first 220 with this speeding bullet beginning to gain ground on me.

As I got half way around the 440 track, Mark was right on my tail when all of a sudden I ran off the track. There was this huge bush-like tree on the side of the track where Tim Storey was hiding! I ran off the track right behind this big bush, when out from the other side came a fresh fast runner with skinny legs and a big fro. It was Tim Storey - the imposter! Tim came running around the last 220 to the roar of the crowd, "Storey! Storey! Storey!"

Tim broke the winner's tape and took us to victory over one of the fastest runners around. The crowd went wild. Mark fell over holding his side in laughter as his victory slipped away. It took both of us to beat Mark Sponsler, but hey, that's called teamwork!

Skinny Dipping!

After a party one night, several of us decided to go down to the high school swimming pool to go swimming. Kerry, Sandy, Frank, Tom, the twin sisters, Tim Storey, and Nina, the beautiful foreign exchange student who Tim had a major crush on, headed down towards the school.

One by one we all took turns jumping the fence to get into the pool area. Without hesitation, everyone disrobed and jumped into the pool, everyone except Tim, Nina, and me. As the crew were all swimming around in their birthday suits, the three of us looked on from a distance and said to each other, those guys are crazy! The next thing you knew, Nina, the unbelievably beautiful blond girl from Finland looked at Tim and me and said, "I'm going in!"

Nina got in her birthday suit right in front of Tim and me, almost causing us to have cardiac arrests at a young age. As she stepped into the pool, she turned and floated away from us like a dream come true for any young red-blooded American male.

I took one look at Tim and proceeded to break the all time record for the fastest undressing in history. Splash! I was in! Tim looked at me as if to say, "Marty, you're crazy." Then Tim decided to,

wait, hold on for a minute, my cell phone is ringing as I write this!

The Toothpaste Story

One weekend a bunch of us guys, including Tim Storey, decided to go camping up north. We all piled into a few cars and headed towards Bishop, California. We were not the seasoned campers; on the contrary, we were a bunch of city slickers! I remember one night in the woods when we were up telling scary stories in the dark. The sounds and noises from the surrounding forest were enough to put the fright in us.

After a long while, one of the guys said it was lights out, time to go to sleep. We all got ready to get into our respective sleeping bags when I decided to pull a joke on Tim. I reached in my bag and pulled out the biggest tube of toothpaste you ever saw. You know...the tubes that look like they could supply tooth brushing for a hundred people. I slipped the tube of toothpaste into Tim's sleeping bag while he went to the "public restroom" in the forest.

When he came back, all of us guys were in our sleeping bags already. Tim lay down, entering his sleeping bag, ready to relax into a restful sleep. All of a sudden he felt something crawl up the side of his leg, as he would tell the story. With a scream of terror that probably frightened every living creature in the woods, Tim jumped up and wrestled his sleeping bag yelling, "There's a snake in my sleeping bag!"

He flew out of the sleeping bag in record time, totally scared of the large Anaconda! All of the guys started cracking up when they saw Tim panic. I went and pulled out the tube of toothpaste from his sleeping bag and said, "Is this the snake you are afraid of?" Needless to say we all busted up that night watching Tim Storey freak out over a tube of Crest! I wonder if he got a good night's sleep after that.

Pizza After The Football Games!

After the high school games, we would all meet up at Me & Ed's Pizza Parlor. This was a favorite local hangout that served some of the best pizza in town. While sitting with Tim, my brother Eric, and the guys, minding our own business, Tim made eye contact with two big white guys sitting on the other side of the pizza parlor.

With no warning, Tim Storey stood up and yelled at the guys and said, "Hey, what are you dudes looking at?" We instantly thought, *Oh no, Tim's going to get us into a fight.* Tim said again standing tall and acting tough, "I said, what are you dudes looking at?" The intimidated guys responded, "Nothing man, it's cool!" They were scared.

The next thing we saw was Tim Storey approaching the two guys causing all of us to sit up, ready to break into a fight. All of a sudden Tim starts shaking hands with these guys like a smooth politician. Always the smooth talker, Tim was now making new friends with the guys he just got done scaring! We all said to ourselves right after, *Good thing Tim made them his friends - because they probably would have kicked our butts!*

From Tennis to Track

One of our all-time favorite stories was when Tim and I were seniors at Monte Vista High School. I wanted to get my varsity letter so I could get a letterman's jacket and strut the halls with Tim Storey and all of the other varsity lettermen.

Tim, who was an awesome varsity tennis player already, invited me to try out for the tennis team. Within minutes I found myself practicing with all of the freshmen and sophomores. Tim was over on the other side of the courts practicing with the seniors and varsity players. It took me about ten minutes to realize, *I am not going to get my varsity letter in tennis.* So without Tim knowing anything, I went up to coach Ed and said, "Coach, I quit!" I ran down to the track where my friend Tom and the track team were starting their first practice. All this time, Tim was hitting tennis balls thinking I was on the other tennis court adjacent to where he was practicing.

The track coach told us all to take a few laps around the tennis courts. The next thing you knew, Tim Storey saw a group of runners coming towards him with me leading the pack. As we ran right by the tennis court, Tim shouted, "Hey Marty, what are you doing?" I yelled out, "Tim, I quit tennis and went out for track!"

Tim began to laugh hysterically along with the other tennis players, and says I will forever be known as the guy who went from one sport to another faster than anyone. I did get my letter in track by the way, while Tim Storey dominated the tennis courts that year!

That's Marty, The One Holding His Side!

I was scheduled to run the mile race in the league track and field finals. It was a beautiful sunny day in Southern California. Tim Storey told me he was going to bring his sister Peggy (who changed her name to Paige several years later) to the track event so I could meet her for the very first time.

There was a small hill that led up to the track from the parking lot where we would be running. The mile run was about to begin when all of us runners took our mark. The mile race was four laps around a 440 yard track that had to be run at a semi-sprint. As we all came around the first lap, I began to drop back a little because my side started to ache. In track and field, this was known as a side-ache. As the fourth and final lap began, I found myself in second to the last place, barely running at a slow jog. I had acquired the worst side-ache ever, and because I was not a quitter, I proceeded to hobble down the track. (Just a side note: I still can't believe there was someone behind me poised to take last place!)

Someone had told me that if you get a side-ache, it would help you if you dug your hand into your side while running. Needless to say it worked a little; however, it sure was a funny sight to see.

Just as I was rounding the last 220 yards, looking like an old hobbling man in trouble, Tim and his beautiful sister Peggy came walking over the hill where the track came into view. Tim said to his sister, "Look Peggy, that's my friend Marty!" I tried to wave to them and almost fell over! They were laughing hysterically - so much that they began to hold *their* sides!

To this day we laugh at this story because the very first time Tim's sister ever saw me was when I was hunched over with my hand in my side, trying desperately to cross the finish line. Well I did finish the race, a little embarrassed as you can imagine.

Tim, in his usual encouragement style, said, "Hey Marty, at least you didn't quit!"

Mr. Personality

I remember Tim Storey being the most likable person in the school. We were at a high school party one night after a football game, and I was standing with some of the guys drinking a bottle of beer with a cigarette in my hand. (I do not endorse this behavior.) Looking back, I can see that Tim had a unique anointing on his life at an early age.

I remember seeing him standing in the middle of a crowd, not drinking at all while everyone else was, and just making everyone laugh with his humorous personality. He never drank alcohol or smoked cigarettes trying to be cool like the rest of us. What I remember is how everyone loved Tim and wanted to be his friend. He was Mr. Personality from a very early age. It's funny to think that Tim was voted "Biggest Gossiper" the year we graduated; he just loved to talk up a storm!

Looking back from today, I think it was more than just personality with Tim - I think it was the call of God upon his life.

"Sometimes you have to step forward before you can step into God's best."

-Tim Storey

Graduation Disco Party

The last week of high school was really fun. Tim and I and a bunch of girls went to Grad Night at Disneyland and tore up the dance floor. The last night of the week, Tim and I were hosting a big disco graduation dance party at my parents' house. (You have to understand that our whole senior class was anti-disco at the time.)

With Tim's influence and my parents being out of town, we threw the best party of the year! We got everyone dancing, especially all of the athletes who were too cool for disco. This was the beginning of the disco years that were soon to follow.

Years later at a few of our high school reunions, everyone cheered when Tim Storey, who was a great dancer, and I, who could bust a few moves, walked into the reunion dinner. They shouted, "Come on Storey and Celaya! Get the party started!" Well, you know we did, and everyone danced the night away. P.S. Tim Storey could spin four times around with his disco moves! Could he still do it today? Perhaps with a push!

"Step up to the spoken prophecy over your life."

Tim Storey

The Mormon Dance

This is a really short story of one night in high school when Tim and I were bored. We decided to crash the dance we heard about at the local Mormon Church. We thought, *Maybe we can meet some girls who like to dance!* Not being Mormons, we were not quite sure what to expect.

We were wearing regular shirts and Levis as we entered - big mistake! All of the young Mormon teenagers were wearing suits, ties, and dresses. As we tried to sneak in incognito, we were apprehended by the Mormon police! (Actually it was the parents who were in charge.) They said that the only way we could go in was to go over to the "Tie Table" and pick out a tie to wear.

As you can imagine, the ties looked like Christmas ornaments with their screaming loud colors. They were those big fat ties that my grandfather's father wore. We each found a tie and laughed at each other as we put them on. Well, we ended up dancing with the girls all night; unfortunately the girls kept asking us where we got our ties! Sometimes you just have to go with the program, even if it means wearing the world's ugliest ties!

"Slow down to the speed of life."

Tim Storey

The Instigator

Okay, so Tim Storey and I are driving down La Mirada Boulevard on a sunny day. As I am driving in my old blue Ford Pinto - you remember...the one that used to blow up because of the bad gas tanks - Tim decided to stir it up a little. We came driving up next to a car where a rather large teenage high schooler dude was driving in the lane next to us. He looked like he was pretty tall and over 200 pounds. He had his girlfriend sitting in the passenger seat as Tim was sitting in my passenger seat.

The next thing you knew, Tim began to wink and flirt with the girl at forty miles an hour! The girl got mad and started yelling and making one finger gestures to Tim, and she wasn't saying you're number one! The guy had his hands on the steering wheel and would not look at Tim if his life depended on it. He looked scared and intimidated, keeping his eyes looking straight forward on the road ahead of him.

At one point, while the crazy ticked off girl and Tim Storey continued their car-to-car conversation, the frightened young driver made the mistake of turning his head to see who this mysterious, flirting, future-world-wide-evangelist was. When the dude and Tim made eye contact, Tim rolled down his window and began screaming at the giant guy saying, "Pull over! Pull over! Pull over!" As I continued driving side by side with the angry girlfriend and her scared-to-death boyfriend, Tim stuck half his body out of the window and was signaling the guy to pull his car over.

Finally their car sped off into the distance while Tim regained his composure, bringing his body back into my car. I remember thinking, *What is Tim doing now? Am I going to get in a fight today?* We both busted up before I asked Tim this question. I said, "Tim, what would you have done if the guy would have pulled his car over?" Tim with his big shiny grin said, "We would have got our butts kicked Marty!" It was then that I looked at Tim thinking to myself, *Oh that's great, just great!*

"Get the bounce back in your life."

Tim Storey

Chapter Two

Kings of the Disco!

Disco Duds!

After turning our high school into a "Disco School," Tim and I moved on to our respective universities, or shall I say junior colleges. Tim went to Fullerton J.C. while I went to Rio "Harvard on the Hill." (Actually, it's Rio Hondo Junior College.) That first year out of high school was fun.

Every weekend there were house disco parties where people would come from all over to strut their stuff. You would receive at least three to four invitations on a Friday at school for the weekend disco extravaganzas! I don't say that lightly. I mean people would fix their homes up like disco clubs, complete with lights, music, food, and the disco ball of course. You would even have to pay a small cover charge to get in.

We would go from the Fullerton College disco parties to the Rio Hondo College parties all in one night! It was pure clean fun where people danced all night to the tunes of MJ and all the other funky beats. Our Disco Duds were complete with fake handkerchiefs, Angel's Flight suits, dancing shoes with clear heels called Crayons, and skinny ties that we bought at the thrift stores. We would spend like an hour getting ready because we thought we were so cool.

I remember Tim Storey taping up his pant cuffs with masking tape several times because he didn't have time to get them tailored. One time as he was into his third spin to Michael Jackson's, "Don't Stop Till You Get Enough," the tape started unraveling right there on the dance floor! That was funny.

Skinny Ties!

The disco apparel was definitely a major part of the cool factor back in the day. Along with doing our best to look like John Travolta straight out of "Saturday Night Fever," it was very important to wear the right "skinny tie."

Tim and I would make the weekly drive to CHOC's Thrift Store in Santa Fe Springs, California. It was here that you could purchase a bag of skinny ties from the sixties era - which were the style - for one dollar. Each bag had about fifteen ties wrapped in a covered bag. Part of the mystery was that you did not know what you would get in each bag. It was kind of like playing the lottery. The goal was to find just one perfect skinny tie per bag.

We generally hit our goal finding at least one skinny tie each for the upcoming weekend of disco mania. With our Angel's Flight suits and our disco shoes, it was crucial to sport the right skinny ties - and we did!

The Charity Dance!

Part of the fun was going from one dance club to the next. On the west side of town, Dillon's Downtown Westwood was a hot spot located by UCLA. This place had four floors and was always packed out with people busting their moves all night long!

On the east side of town there were places like The Crescendo. This popular club was a little classier than many other places. I mean we really had to have our cool on at this place. Then there was Circle City, the Orange County disco club where the East met the West! Tim and I would walk in and demand respect; after all we were disco legends - in our own minds.

Because we were the coolest of the coolest, we decided to be generous and allow one lonely girl the incredible opportunity to have one very special dance with us. This was known as "The Charity Dance." At some point in the evening, Tim and I would look at each other and say, "It's time." We would then proceed to search the room for the loneliest unattractive girl - usually the one sitting all by herself off in the corner.

I remember, Tim and I would walk up to these girls and say in a polite way, "Would you like to dance?" The thrill of watching these girls light up with excitement was well worth the cause. We would bless them with our dance and our presence, take them back to their respective corners, and then Tim and I would share our ministry experiences with each other about how we blessed and impacted these girls for the common good. It wasn't until later on that Tim and I learned the real meaning of charity, but up until that time, it was all about "The Charity Dance."

Tim's Unlucky Night

I'll never forget the night at the Circle City disco club. The atmosphere was electric and everyone was dressed to impress. I was sitting at the table sipping a soda with a girl I had been dancing with throughout the night.

There were a few other couples sitting at the same table along with Tim. He stood up and said, "I'll be right back. I'm going to go find me a cute girl to dance and hang out with."

Now keep in mind, we were 19 years old at the time. After a while, Tim came back to the table with this striking brunette who, I must say, had a really pretty smile. As we sat there for a moment, all of a sudden the cute girl placed her right hand up on the table. Wow! We were taken back as we all noticed Miss Beautiful was missing a few fingers! The look on Tim's face was priceless and worth the gas money that night.

Tim proceeded to take the girl away from our table only to return a few minutes later with another cute girl. This one was blond with a super nice outfit as I recall. Tim and Blondie sat down with our group when Tim said, "Hey you guys, I would like you all to meet Julie." One of us said, "Hi Julie. Where are you from?" Julie responded, "What?" Turns out she was deaf! I looked at Tim and he gave me a sad look as to say, *This is my unlucky night.*

"Your self-worth should be greater than your performance."

Tim Storey

The Anointing at Dillon's Downtown Westwood

I remember the Sunday night at Dillon's disco when God showed up in the middle of a Rick James funky song. We had started going to First Family Church in Whittier, California for the Sunday morning service. We would sit in church talking about which club we would hit that night. We were not that strong in our faith at the time.

Tim's Sister Peggy was on fire for God and was full of the Holy Spirit. I remember how Peggy had the biggest Bible in the world, and she would say to Tim and me, "You guys can't do church in the mornings and then go disco dancing at night!" In spite of the conviction we felt, that Sunday night, Dillon's was the place of choice.

Tim asked this girl to dance while I stood back and watched from a distance. What I remember to this day was seeing Tim's face as he busted out. He seemed a bit serious and compassionate while doing all of his disco moves. He almost had tears in his eyes as he danced with this girl. Later, Tim told me how he felt God's presence right there on the dance floor as he felt compassion for the young lady. He actually said he thought about her eternal destiny right in the middle of the disco.

It's just like God to show up where we least expect Him! Tim then finished the dance strong by doing his signature four spin move with watery eyes and compassion in his heart. Tim Storey - always caring about people.

Drama at Tommy's Burgers in L.A.

Another great memory for me was standing in the long line at 2:00 A.M. waiting to sink my big teeth into a few Tommy's burgers. Every time Tim and I would go to the dance clubs in the Los Angeles area, we never failed to stop at the world famous original Tommy's burgers on the way home. If you've never experienced a Tommy's burger, you have not truly lived!

Well the truth is you either love them or you hate them. All I know is that we were amongst the true Tommy's burger believers who were willing to wait out the long lines just to have that big burger with the chili sauce. (I am actually getting hungry as I write this!) After eating the hamburgers, the smell of the chili would stay on your hands for at least two days - I'm serious!

One night, while standing in line behind this real big American-Indian-looking dude, Tim started asking him questions about who he was and where he was from. The big guy was cool and told us he lived there in the neighborhood and was a long-time Tommy's regular. All of a sudden, these four guys, out of nowhere, walked through the line and cut right in front of Tim, me, and the giant Indian. As they got their food, they walked past us again making a smart remark to the big dude.

Big mistake! The guys had gotten into their car when the big Indian went over and yanked one of them out. He began to slam the guy on the hood of the car while his frightened buddies sat in fear watching from the vehicle. After putting a serious hurt on the guy, he let him go as they hauled out of the parking lot. The gigantic Indian guy wearing a long trench-type coat rejoined us in the line.

Tim Storey said to him, "What would you have done if all four of those guys would have jumped you?" The big Indian pulled back his coat and showed us his hand gun which he had on his hip. He said, "No problem, I would have used this!" Tim and I got our hamburgers and nervously left the premises.

Would You Like To Dance?

One of the funny stories that Tim always asks me to tell from our disco days is the night at Crescendo, the classy club (if you've been reading). We all walked in as the music was bumping and took our rightful places up against the wall.

Let me explain and paint the scene.

About fifty guys all GQ'd out would stand on one side of the room holding up the wall. All of the beautiful girls would sit at the round tables in front of us and close to the dance floor.

Always the instigator, trying to stir something up, Tim said to me. "Hey Marty, why don't you ask one of those girls over there to dance?" I think Tim had the gift of discernment knowing what was about to happen. I boldly stepped out in representation of all the guys and began my long walk through the round tables all the way up to the very last table next to the dance floor.

As I walked the walk that would later become known as the "Walk of Shame," I knew that all eyes were on me. There were four young disco girls sitting at the table. Like a gentleman, I asked the first girl if she would like to dance. Tim's version from his perspective is remembering me stretch out my hand to the young lady, only to see her shake her head, "No thanks." Tim remembers watching me crash and burn as I repeated the outstretched hand to the next three girls.

One by one they each said they were either tired or that their feet hurt. As I stood there dejected and rejected, I knew I would have to turn around and walk all the way back to the wall with a sense of shame in front of the other forty-nine guys who allowed me to be the guinea pig. Tim, in his usual encouragement way said, "Marty, at least you had the guts to make the first move!" I felt better after that. It was the other 9,000 times in later years when Tim made me tell this story to the laughs of everyone that I still cope with! Just kidding.

"God wants you to live an Utmost Life."

Tim Storey

Chapter Three

On Fire for God!

Leading Me to Christ!

At the age of 20, and after a few years of disco fever, my life was about to change because of my good friend, Tim Storey. Tim had grown up in the church and always maintained his relationship with the Lord. One day Tim stepped out by faith and invited me to his home church, First Family Church in Whittier, California.

I was raised Catholic but really never attended much church growing up. This church in Whittier was a Pentecostal Assemblies of God church where people really appeared to love God. Tim took me right down to sit in the fourth row on the right. After the singing and the preaching, I felt the Holy Spirit in a way I had never experienced before.

It was on that Sunday that I accepted Jesus Christ formally at the altar and began a life-long journey of serving Christ. I will always be grateful to Tim Storey who invited me to his church at a young age, and had the guts to not be ashamed of his faith. Thanks Tim Storey!

What's He Going To Do With That?

When it comes to joking around, the location really never has been an issue for Tim. One day on a Sunday while attending First Family Church as a brand new Christian, I was sitting next to Tim Storey during the service.

As the offering plate was being passed down the aisle, I reached deep down into my pocket and pulled out a handful of change to put into the offering plate. I remember being so sincere with the feeling like, *God, I'm going to give you everything I have!*

As Tim handed me the plate, I dropped all of the change I had as an offering with a heart of compassion and love. Tim took one look at me and said, "What's He going to do with that?!" I was so sad.

Learning the Word

One of Tim's good friends from childhood who remains a brother to this day is Don Comotofski. Donny has known Tim longer then me; I believe since they were nine or ten years old. I got to know Donny after the high school years and sometimes hung around him and Tim.

About the time when Tim brought me to church, Donny was on fire for God and had a heart for missions. I remember back in the day when Tim, Donny and I would drive around in the car playing the scripture quote game. Each one of us would take turns quoting a scripture verse until one of us drew a blank. This would mean having to quit the game while the other two battled it out for bragging rights!

The truth is every time we would start, I would be the first one ejected from the game.

Tim Storey and Brother Donny were on fire in their faith and were scripture memorizing machines. I remember getting so mad because these guys would constantly kill me in this game that I decided to memorize the Word with the sole intention of destroying these modern day disciples! Well, I remember the day when I was the last man standing and it felt so good to finally defeat these two world shakers for God.

As we finished the game and I soaked up a moment of victory, Tim said, "You guys want to go to Jack in the Box for a hamburger?" My victory was short lived, yet I owe some thanks to Tim and Don for their efforts to help me learn the word.

"Give the Lord a shout."

Tim Storey

Filled With the Holy Spirit!

I was sitting at the Carriage Cafe in La Mirada, California with Tim Storey and a guy named Kevin. Kevin was a friend of Tim's older sister Peggy and was totally on fire for God. Kevin was telling Tim and me about being baptized in the Holy Spirit with the evidence of speaking in tongues. (This is all in the Bible, by the way.)

Tim and I listened intently to Kevin describe his own experience when suddenly Tim Storey blurted out, "I want to receive this baptism in the Holy Spirit right now!" We quickly left the cafe and drove in a hurry to Tim's house.

For the next few hours the three of us prayed and sought the Lord intently in the middle of Bessie Storey's living room, asking the Lord to fill us with His power. I will never forget witnessing Tim Storey being filled with God's supernatural power as he began to speak in tongues.

It was as though the heavens opened up right before our eyes! The Spirit of God was so strong in the room, you felt like you could cut it with a knife. Several minutes later I began to speak in tongues being filled by God's Spirit. This was a defining moment in our lives that empowered us to make a difference for Christ. It was during that time when God began a new journey in the lives of two hungry young men, filling us with His power. From that point on, we became radical for Christ.

The First Bible Study

One of my best memories as a new Christian was the Friday night Bible studies at Tim Storey's house. A bunch of us would meet in Bessie Storey's living room for powerful times of worship and prayer. We all were attending First Family Church under the ministry of Pastor Ron Prinzing at that time.

The Bible study became a place where many friends and non-believers would come and experience God for the first time! It was like a gateway to getting many people plugged in to the church. It was here that Tim Storey began to teach and preach, developing his gifts and talents, right in the middle of the living room with about 30 people.

Many of us got a chance to teach the Friday night Bible studies which became a foundation for many future teaching ministries. I remember some of Tim's greatest messages being birthed in a Friday night Bible study on Kibbie Street.

The Power Hit! Somebody Catch Greg!

It was in the Friday night Bible studies that I first began to witness this unbelievable power and anointing on Tim Storey's life. After he would teach the word and fire us all up, he began to lay hands on us as the Bible says to do.

Oh my goodness! People started receiving the Baptism in the Holy Spirit, people were healed, and many of our old party friends got saved right on the spot. I'll never forget the night when our old buddy, Greg Sandoval, got prayed for by Tim.

Greg was Mr. Integrity as I remember, and was one of the most conservative dudes in the church. I was young in my faith at that time, so I was a little skeptical of this power thing! Tim full of boldness said, "Greg, get over here! Close your eyes and lift your hands." Greg conservatively followed Tim's direction as Tim laid his hand on Greg's head.

Tim said, "Now!" All of a sudden, I kid you not, Greg flew across the room as though he had stuck his hand in a light socket! People in the room began to weep and cry out to God for more of a demonstration of His spirit. I stood there in shock like a child who just saw a ghost! *Oh my God!* I said to myself, *This is for real. That must be God!* Well that was the first time I saw someone "fall out under the Spirit" as we say, but it wouldn't be the last.

"Reach up and pull down your miracle."

Tim Storey

In Shock!

I remember when Tim worked for a period of time years ago helping mentally challenged young people. There was an incident by the swimming pool where one of the children somehow ended up on the bottom of the pool. As I recall, Tim told me he jumped in, swam to the bottom and brought the kid up by the arm. The child was already turning blue as they laid him on the deck.

Tim laid hands on this child and prayed, "In the name of Jesus, be healed!" The young person appeared to be lifeless as the paramedics quickly arrived. They took over and revived this child, later telling Tim that the child had not been breathing. They communicated to Tim that they did not think this child should be alive.

What I honestly remember was Tim coming over to my house soon after this incident took place. I remember his face, almost in shock as he told me what happened. Whether you believe that this child was raised from the dead is not the issue; what I know is that Tim prayed over this child who had been in the water for several minutes, and the authorities said it was a miracle. It was the power of God flowing through the prayer of faith that I believe saved that child.

"Your current ceiling will become the floor of your next level."

Tim Storey

It's Time Meetings - The Birth of Forceful Men

As time went on and we began to grow as young on-fire Christians, Tim decided to start a Thursday night men's Bible study in the same living room where we had the Friday night Bible studies in his mom's house.

I remember about 30 to 40 guys started coming from many different churches. We had the Calvary Chapel guys, the Pentecostal brothers, and a whole bunch of men who attended different local churches.

I recently had coffee with my old friend Dave Hartel who attended a Calvary church. We met at a local Starbucks. I haven't seen Brother Dave for over twenty years, and it was a blessing to hear him ask me if I remembered the old Thursday night meetings. We also had a lot of our old neighborhood buddies who came and got saved in these meetings. It was here that Tim

Storey taught us and cast so much vision into our lives causing us to want to save the world!

Tim would allow some of the older guys like our dear friend Ron Gabriel, who is now in heaven, to teach us how to be men of God. As I reflect back on those days, I realize how special it was for many of us to be a part of such a dynamic group.

About seven years later, as I recall, Tim hosted one of the greatest conferences in America at that time. It was called "The Forceful Men & Women Conference" at Phoenix First Assembly of God Church. Pastor Tommy Barnett opened up his great church where thousands of people attended from all around the world. The greatest speakers all assembled in one place. Reinhard Bonnke from Africa, Benny Hinn, The Power Team, Carmen, Tommy Barnett, Ron Prinzing, and many other world shakers shared the stage with Tim Storey.

This conference shook the nation and changed the lives of many. Many more great ministry experiences were to come, but what I remember is how the Forceful Men & Women Conference was birthed out of a little men's group in La Mirada, California by an on-fire young dreamer named Tim Storey.

"Don't nurse it, curse it, rehearse it, but let God reverse it."

Tim Storey

Marty Hinn!

One thing I've always liked about Tim Storey is his ability to think quickly at the moment. We were all having a great time at the Forceful Men and Women Conference in Phoenix, Arizona. The featured speaker that night was world renowned evangelist, Benny Hinn.

I had been hanging out with Tim Storey and Benny's brother Henry Hinn immediately following the service. We decided to meet at the hotel hot tub over by the big swimming pool to relax. Tim, Henry and I were sitting in the hot tub when a group of girls got in the hot water.

They had just attended the service with Benny Hinn, the great evangelist. The girls recognized Tim Storey who was the conference host, and they new who Henry was. The girls chatted up a storm asking Tim and Henry a million questions a minute! For fifteen minutes I sat there watching these star-struck girls ramble on. All of a sudden, out of left field, Tim said to the girls, "You know Henry Hinn, but have you met Benny and Henry's brother, Marty Hinn?" I just smiled and went with the program for a few minutes.

The next thing I remember was these girls wanting to talk to me all of a sudden. How funny is that?! Tim did not skip a beat and played it off like the master joke teller he can be. On the way back to our rooms, I said "Tim, you are too funny, man." Tim replied, "Well at least they talked to you! And by the way, you can pass for a Hinn brother any day of the week!" We all shared a laugh that night.

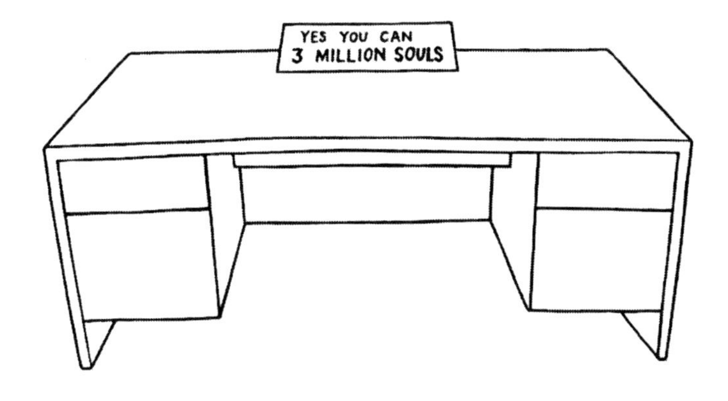

Yes You Can! Three Million Souls!

I still remember to this day the inspiring faith that Tim displayed as a young 19 year old. Tim created a small sign that he put on his desk that said, "Yes You Can! Three Million Souls!" Back then it was a little hard for me to envision such a large dream, but Tim Storey saw it before it became a reality! His faith was so strong that he went on to seeing this dream fulfilled probably several times over through a life-long service and ministry to the Lord. Tim would always say, "You have to believe it, see it, and then achieve it." To this day Tim inspires me to believe God for the best. Thanks buddy.

"Don't sit in your setback. Prepare for your comeback."

Tim Storey

Dr. Yonggi Cho at Melodyland Christian Center

In the early days, we were so hungry for the word of God that we would go anywhere just to learn and get under the spout where the Glory was coming out!

A wonderful memory was being with Tim Storey and our good friend Donny at Melodyland. This church had a famous reputation for hosting the greatest ministers and ministries in the world. We heard that Paul Yonggi Cho, who later changed his name to David Paul, and who was the Pastor of the huge church in Seoul Korea, was coming to Melodyland.

I will never forget us three young hungry tigers soaking up the message Dr. Cho preached on. I still remember to this day that he spoke on the "Waters of Marah." He taught us about not having bitterness in our hearts. Years later I was blessed to hear another great minister preach many times at Melodyland Christian Center; it was Tim Storey.

"You are the head and not the tail, above and not beneath, your going over and not under."

Tim Storey

You Will Be An Evangelist and Win Souls Around The World!

I remember when Tim asked me to go to a service at Melodyland to hear a great preacher and prophet named Dick Mills. Dick Mills had been doing several services that week, and for some reason I didn't go to the one I'm going to share with you.

I was fortunate to have Reverend Mills confirm this story first-hand to me when he spoke at one of my Full Gospel Businessmen lunches years later. What I remember is Tim telling me right after about how God called him out of the crowd to be an evangelist that would win souls around the world!

As the story goes, Dick Mills was preaching and stopped in the middle of his message, looked up into the crowd and made eye contact with Tim Storey. Dick Mills said, "You, young man," looking right at Tim, "The Lord Jesus Christ is calling you to be an evangelist, and you will win souls around the world!" Tim almost fell out of his seat when he realized that the anointed minister was speaking to him.

"Bam!" as Tim would say. God was specifically giving him a call out of hundreds of people about what was to take place in the future. Tim was overwhelmed that God would call him out so specifically. Well, as we all know, the rest became and continues to become history.

"Sometimes you have to get left in order to go right."

Tim Storey

"God Put the Country of Sweden On My Heart."

Before I tell you one of the greatest stories which have wonderfully affected my life and so many others, let me say it's interesting that I'm writing this while on vacation in Stockholm, Sweden, many years after this took place.

As a young, on-fire man of God, Tim Storey left to Florida to attend South Eastern Bible College. Tim tells many stories about his early bible school years, including this one, in many other books he has written.

It was a summer night when Tim came back to Southern California during his school break. One night we sat in my car eating tacos in front of a popular fast food place. I'll never forget Tim saying to me, "Hey Marty, God has put the country of Sweden on my heart!" I said "Switzerland?" He said "No, Sweden!" Switzerland, Sweden, it was all the same to me. We were two young guys from Southern California who had not traveled too much. Well, actually Tim had gone a few places, but I had never been farther than our neighboring city.

He began to say that God was giving him a burden for the people of Sweden. Tim returned to bible school and as the story goes, something interesting was about to happen. A well known leader and preacher named Barbara Valin came from Sweden to speak at Tim's school for their chapel service. After the service was over, Tim was asked to drive Barbara Valin to the airport. All of a sudden Barbara said to young Tim Storey, "The Holy Spirit is telling me that you must come to my country young man!" Wow! After God had impressed Tim with this burden, he was now being invited to Sweden.

Tim came home again and shared this blessing with his family and friends. I was a young construction worker at the time living at home with a lot of money in my pocket. The Lord spoke to me and put on my heart to pay for Tim's first overseas flight to Sweden. I proceeded to pay the first and second trip for Tim back in the day. To this day Tim has always honored me for this.

Tim went on and preached and ministered in Sweden as God began to open up the nations for him. Tim Storey has since been to Sweden so many times, it is hard to count! He is still having a positive dynamic influence in Sweden to this day. I must say that these were the first of many nations where God has used the ministry gifts and talents of Tim Storey.

If I may share from my perspective, the number of lives that have been changed, and the number of ministries which have been birthed regarding Sweden is incredible. I, for one, have been honored and privileged to minister in this country many times over the years, and I also have been blessed with two wonderful Swedish-American children in my life after marrying a wonderful Swedish woman. Someone once said, "You go where you sow!" Well, I have certainly been blessed in so many ways with the Swedish connection, and it's all because a young on-fire-for-God dreamer named Tim Storey had the guts and faith to step out and believe that with God, all things are possible. Thanks again, Tim.

"You are a world shaker and

a history maker."

Tim Storey

Katrina

I remember sitting at the table in Tim's mother's house one night when we were about 19 years old. We were on fire for God wanting to save the world at that time. Tim had a phone number written on a little piece of paper from a girl we had met named Katrina. Katrina was a very nice girl who struggled with split personalities. I had only seen the side of her that was well mannered and calm; however, Tim had told me that she would change into a completely different person. He told me that she would become a prostitute who would act completely bizarre.

Tim crumpled up the paper with her phone number on it and threw it across the room into the trash can, when the Holy Spirit spoke to him to go get the paper out of the trash. It was the Holy Spirit telling Tim that we needed to try to help this 18 year old girl. We called Katrina so that we could get her into a halfway house for girls.

We met with her and took her shopping just trying to help her out with some clothes. After getting her into a place called Hope for Hollywood, a Christian home to help girls like Katrina, Tim received a call one night from Katrina telling him she ran away from the half way house. When we found her I was completely blown away at the girl I saw. She had transformed into a prostitute with a different personality and attitude. We again tried to persuade her to go back to the home, but she ran away from us.

The next morning Tim received a call from Katrina who told him she had spent the night in a motel with some dude she didn't even know. She told Tim that she left the motel and took the guys clothes - all of them! We ended up helping Katrina into a mental facility where we would go to see her from time to time. It was sad to see this girl and our hearts went out to her.

Tim and I were two young guys who just wanted to make a difference, and we both felt a whole lot of compassion towards Katrina. We lost contact with her, but I will never forget Tim throwing a little paper into the trash, only to hear God's voice asking us to help Katrina. It's just like God to leave the 99 and to go after the 1!

Chased By The Pimp!

We used to drive all the way to Hollywood to witness to the prostitutes and the pimps. Sunset Boulevard was always a place where hundreds of people would come out to cruise the road and walk the streets. One night as Tim and I were driving down Sunset Boulevard, we would take turns witnessing, or sharing the love of Christ with the prostitutes who would stand on the corner.

As Tim was driving, I said, "Pull over up ahead. I'll get that one." There was a young "lady of the night" standing on the corner. Tim approached the corner. Passing the girl. he turned right and parked the car. Tim said, "Go on, I'll wait for you." I got out of the car and walked up the block to the corner where the girl was. I said, "Excuse me, I just want you to know that Jesus loves you." She was quite gracious and said, "Thank you so much, but I'm working right now." Just then I looked up and made eye contact with this huge black dude in a big pimp coat. He took one look at me and then started to run right towards me across the street! I said to the girl, "Oh shoot! God bless you! Gotta go!" I started running around the corner being chased by the biggest, meanest, ugliest pimp in the world! (Well, I added a few more words to spice up the story.)

Okay, back to the story. So as I come running around the corner, the pimp is right behind me. I start yelling, "Tim, Tim, start the car!" It's a good thing Tim was watching in his rear view mirror. Tim started the car, threw open the door, and started driving away without me, yelling, "Get in! Get in!" With the angry pimp just inches behind me, I had to literally throw myself into a moving car as Tim Storey sped away. We were a little shaken up - well at least I was - before calming down. We then shared a huge laugh as we headed towards the next corner; after all, it was Tim's turn next.

"You are a work in progress."

Tim Storey

Leading My Brother Eric to The Lord

After a few years being in the church and growing in God from our Friday night Bible studies, I had been witnessing to my brother Eric about Jesus for many months. He was quite resistant to the gospel message, and it frustrated me every time I would witness to him. Eric was attending college and was always the intellectual one in the family.

One day I came home to find my brother being led to Christ by my friend Tim Storey. I was happy on the one hand, but felt a little cheated because I did all the work. How selfish and ridiculous is that?! We all know that it is the Holy Spirit who really does the work! Well, Tim was obedient in sharing the Gospel with my brother and later included Eric as a board member of his ministry.

My brother is an unbelievably awesome person today with a wonderful Godly family. I am so proud of him. Thanks Tim for never giving up with my family and for coming to our house that day.

Our New Singles Pastor

In 1985, Tim Storey became our singles Pastor at First Family Church in Whittier, California. It was such an awesome group of people, and we loved sitting under the ministry of this dynamic on-fire dreamer!

Tim had some great messages such as, "Walking in Love," "Slavery has been Abolished," "Come to where the Giants Roam," just to name a few. So many of us learned and were influenced by Tim in the early days. I think of a young guy named Benny Perez who patterned his early ministry after Tim Storey.

Benny went on to become a great evangelist and pastor in his own right, but continues to honor Tim with much of his success today. I think of people like Patty, Mike, and Leticia whom I led to Christ. I brought them all to meet Tim and join our group. I remember Mike and Patty telling me years later how they were so impressed with Tim being so down to earth. Mike said he expected to meet this real religious guy, when all of a sudden Tim Storey walked up carrying a boom box with some funky music playing.

Patty remembers Tim being a regular guy she could relate to. Mike and Leticia sat under the ministry of Tim Storey, and a few years later they took over the singles ministry at First Family Church. They went on to become pastors as well. Patty has a wonderful family and still attends this church as a leader to this day. It was a great time for all of us that I will never forget. It was from here that Tim launched out to become a pastor in Texas before hitting the evangelistic trail.

"Hey Marty, Play One of Your Songs!"

We were at a singles retreat up in the mountains during the time that Tim was our singles pastor. I grew up in a home where we had a piano, and I used to write a few songs with the three cords that I knew. They kind of all sounded the same.

The whole singles group, about 150 people came together at the retreat for a time of worship and ministry. As you probably know by now, Tim and I were always playing jokes on each other. This night while everyone was seated, right before the meeting was about to begin, Tim got up in front of the crowd and said, "Tonight we have a special treat. Hey Marty, play one of your songs!" Everyone sat up in their chairs watching to see what I would do. Tim who was thinking that he would embarrass me and get a good laugh, was stunned as I stood up and made my way directly to the piano.

I walked with the swagger of Liberace as though I was a world famous concert pianist! With all eyes on me, I proceeded to play and sing a song I wrote called, "Through the Eyes of You Lord." Immediately following my stellar performance, I arose from the piano bench to a standing ovation! Tim Storey stood in shock as I walked away from the piano back to my seat. That night I gave Tim a look as to say, *Hey buddy, how's that for a treat?!* Tim just stood there shaking his head with the biggest smile you can imagine.

You Know I like Her!

During the time when Tim was leading our singles group, a young, stunningly attractive Hispanic girl joined our class. Along with Bob Gagliano, and many other guys, I immediately was drawn to this Latin beauty and thought to myself, *She's hot!* (Can I be real?) What I didn't know is that she had her eyes on the leader who happened to be my best friend, Tim!

One day after church, we all went to have Mexican food at a local restaurant. After we all ate, we said our goodbyes and I told Tim, "I'll catch you later." As I was heading home, something told me to swing by Tim's house for a moment. I would like to say it was the Holy Spirit, but the truth is it was my jealous nature kicking in.

As I came driving up to Tim's house, I saw the young lady's yellow Volkswagen parked out front. I went up to the front door that was open a little because it was a hot day. I walked in and found Tim and Cindy having some iced tea, engaging in a friendly conversation. I said, "Hey guys, listen, I'll come back later." Tim didn't say a word! I left his house feeling crushed thinking, *Why are you talking to her? You know I like her!*

That week I attended a small group of a few guys from the church. We were being discipled by our long time friend, Pastor Randy. This was a group where anything goes and where we could vent or speak our mind. When it came time for me to speak, Pastor Randy said, "So Marty, what's on your mind?" I jumped up and said in front of the guys, "Tim Storey, I'm so mad at you!" Tim sat there in shock and said, "What did I do?" I said, "You know I like Cindy!" All of the guys in the room couldn't believe what I was saying. Tim said, "It's not my fault. She likes me." They literally had to restrain me from attacking one of our great ministers of our day! We later look back and laugh at this story, especially because Tim and Cindy married and had two great children who call me uncle Marty to this day.

"I Can Do This," Said Tim Storey.

One of the greatest times in my life were the days at First Family Church when Tim Storey was our singles pastor. We always had super fun retreats up in the mountains of Big Bear, California. Because we had such an awesome group of people, we always had a great time of spiritual renewal along with a whole lot of fun!

One of the highlights was snow skiing up at "Snow Summit." Everyone headed out to the slopes to catch the chair lift that would take you all the way up to the top of the mountain. Tim said to me, "Hey Marty, will you show me how to ski over on the beginner's hill?" We broke away from the group and headed for the chair lift line where all of the children were standing. Tim and I tried to fit in, but I don't think it was working! We caught the chair that started to take us up to the top of the beginner's hill. I am tempted to use the word slope, but truth be told it was just a little hill!

After sitting down on the chair lift, we jumped off about thirty seconds later; this gives you an indication of how high up we went. Tim geared up for the first time in his life to conquer the mountain! I said, "Now Tim, watch me as I snow plow." Basically I was telling him and showing him how to come to a stop by pointing the skis together. Tim is such a perfectionist at everything he attempts, therefore he began to go for it all at once.

After a quick wipeout, Tim sprung up with energy and said to himself - not to me, "Come on Tim Storey, you can do this!" With the tenacity of a bull dog, and several falls later, I watched Tim get up after every fall, brush off the snow, put his skis back on, talk to himself, and proceed downhill. Even though the hill was not big, Tim fell at least seven or eight times.

The best part of this story is that Tim got up eight times and eventually skied to the bottom standing up. He was so proud of himself and he had the biggest grin on his face. He said, "Marty, let's do it again!" I said, "Tim, I'm going to go get some hot chocolate!"

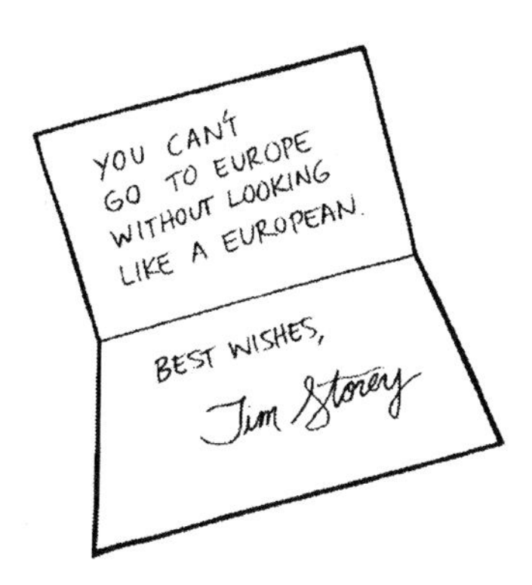

"This Daniel Hetcher Should Help."

Tim Storey has always been such an encourager to me. In 1987, I was given the opportunity to travel to England to preach and teach in several churches and schools. This would be my first overseas trip ever! A few days before I was scheduled to leave, I received a gift package in the mail at my house.

Wondering what this could be (after all it wasn't Christmas or my birthday), I began to open the card. It simply said, "Marty, you can't go to Europe without looking like a European! This Daniel Hetcher should help!" Wow, it was a brand new suit from Tim. I thought this was so cool for him to do this. He really encouraged me and showed me that he believed in me. I went to England and preached up a storm in my new suit everywhere I went. The Brits probably thought, *I wonder if Minister Marty only owns one suit!*

"Before your God given ascension, there will always be an attempted assassination."

Tim Storey

The False Prophet

The story I'm about to share with you is a bit intense. It is one story out of many where spiritual warfare took place. A church near the border of California and Mexico had been praying for two months for the arrival of Tim Storey for their church crusade. These people were so full of faith that I believe the enemy became agitated!

I was sitting in the front row and there were probably 500 people in the crowd that day. Tim began to preach his message flowing in the anointing as usual. The next thing you know, a big man who was dressed like an Amish farmer stood up in the middle of Tim's preaching and said, "I am an evangelist, and I have something to say!"

Tim was quite gracious and asked the big guy to please sit down because he was in the middle of his sermon. Tim told the man in a nice way that he would be happy to speak with him after the service. The big man sat down for about thirty seconds as Tim resumed his message. All of a sudden the farmer-looking guy with a real long beard stood up again and interrupted Tim's preaching.

Tim, being full of discernment, immediately sensed the enemy at work and said to the crowd, "Everyone close your eyes and stretch forth your hands towards this man and pray in the spirit!" As the crowd bowed their heads to pray, the man began to manifest in a demonic way, yelling and cursing with the worst language you can imagine. Immediately, the ushers, who happened to be tough Hispanic border patrol agents, came running up the aisle to attempt to escort the big man and his wife out of the church.

I watched as one usher politely tried to help the man out when the big dude pulled back his arm in an aggressive manner. He said, "Don't *blanking* touch me!" Wrong move! These short stocky border patrol guys physically removed this giant of a man to the back of the church foyer allowing the service to continue. Many lives were touched by God that day.

After the service ended, I sat in the pastor's office with Tim Storey. The pastor said to Tim and me, "Do you want to hear something strange?" He proceeded to tell us that the big farmer and his wife had never been seen by any of the staff before. The ushers told the pastor that when they escorted the man and his wife outside into the parking lot of the church, the strange couple started walking down the highway like two drifters who had wandered into the church service out of nowhere. They had no transportation coming in, and they had no transportation when they left. The pastor then told us that his church had been praying and fasting for the supernatural power of God to be revealed in the upcoming Tim Storey crusade.

We then knew that this was a feeble attempt of the enemy to distract the crusade from the word being spoken and the signs and wonders that were to follow. Tim and I left that crusade experiencing many salvations, healings, blessings, and miracles. On the way home, we discussed what happens when God's people bind together to pray and fast for, in the words of Tim Storey, HIS super to touch our natural! It was truly a supernatural weekend.

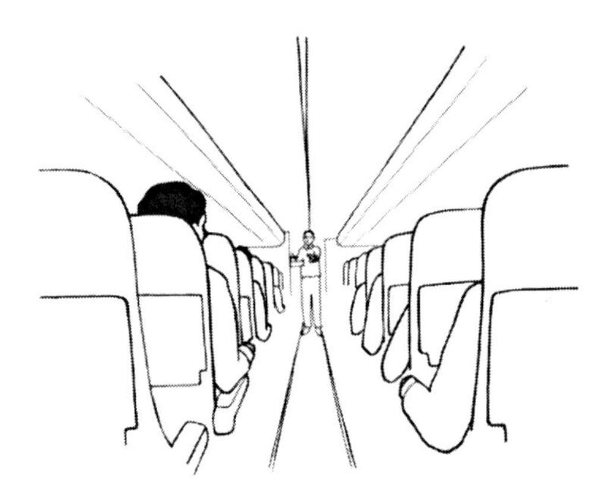

Could You Pass This Down To The Guy In The Back?

It's funny how you can remember different things. I was flying with Tim to some small city I believe in Arizona or Texas, I can't quite recall. What I remember was Tim and me in a tiny little airport waiting for a jumper plane to come and take us to the city where he would be preaching. It was one of those small airports in the middle of "Nowhere, USA," but everyone who worked there seemed to know Tim Storey!

Our small plane arrived; I seem to remember it being a twenty-four seat bird with twelve seats on each side. Tim wanted to order some sandwiches and drinks for the ride, so he told me to go board the plane and that he would catch up. I proceeded to board first and realized that my seat was the very last one in the back of this tiny airship. The next thing I remember is everyone sitting in their seats ready for takeoff, except Tim! There was one seat in the front of the plane which would soon be Tim's.

Tim was taking his time getting the food as he came casually strolling towards the plane. Up the stairs he walked, sticking his head into the plane with his hands filled with food and drink. Everyone clapped their hands as though Tim was the President of the United States. From the back of the plane, I saw Tim's dilemma. *How do I get Marty's food to him?* he pondered in his mind with a slight smile on his face. With quick thinking and the creativity that only Tim Storey could come up with, I watched him hand my food to the person in the first seat. The next thing you know, each person turned around handing my food to the next person behind them, asking them to do the same.

One by one I watched Tim recruit all the passengers in order to get the job done. I sat there and smiled watching my food pass through several hands before it finally reached me. It's a miracle to think that all of my french fries didn't mysteriously disappear! I looked at Tim who was sitting in the front, and he gave me one of those big grins. Well the plane took off, bumpy as can be, and the last thing I remember is spilling my coke all over my pants! Well, you can't win them all!

"Don't consult your past performance to

determine your potential future."

Tim Storey

"I'm Going to Get to Magic!"

I remember over the years how Tim Storey would tell many of us who have been close to him something he believed God was about to do in the future. When the great basketball player Magic from the LA Lakers reported to the world that he had contracted HIV, not long afterward I remember Tim saying to me, "I feel in my spirit that I'm going to get to Magic J. to minister to him."

At the time, it sounded a little far fetched because Tim had no contact with the basketball superstar. A few months later, Tim moved into a condo in Diamond Bar, California, next to a young actor named Chip. When Tim settled into the neighborhood, he got to talking with his new neighbor. It turned out that this guy Chip grew up with Magic and knew him personally.

The next thing I remember is Tim telling me that he was going to Magic's New Year's party and that he would be introduced to the great basketball player. Tim met Magic and became good friends with him. He ministered to him just as the Holy Spirit showed him he would. I learned that when Tim told us something he felt that God was going to do with him, or through him, not to doubt Him. This has been the pattern of Tim's ministry over many years. How awesome is that?!

The Hollywood Bible Study

From around 1995 to 2001, the coolest place to be was at the Hollywood Bible Study. Everyone wanted to be there and it was so much fun. God had spoken to Tim Storey many years earlier that he would minister to the entertainment community, and as you would know it, it came to pass. Tim continues to reach out to the Hollywood elite today helping them with ministry and life coaching.

Back in 1995, Tim and a well known Hollywood actress started a Bible study in her home for a small group of people. As the study grew, it eventually outgrew the home where they were meeting. Tim and our team moved the Hollywood Bible Study over to the Mondrian Hotel on Sunset. Later we would move to the Hilton and the Wyndam Belage Hotel. The word started to get out that this dynamic, positive, motivational preacher was holding monthly meetings for the entertainment industry.

It wasn't long before many of the top entertainers in all of Hollywood, whose names I cannot mention because there are too many, started coming on a regular basis. The Hollywood Bible Study became a safe place and a refuge for these entertainers, producers, actors, directors, and everyone else related to the industry.

One night I was sitting next to Tim in the front row, minutes before the Bible Study was about to begin. Tim looked to the left and did a double take. He looked at me and said, "Marty, is that Natalie Cole sitting over there?" Of course you know Natalie Cole is a very famous singer. I looked and said, "Oh my goodness, it is Natalie. Do you know her Tim?" He said, "No." The ushers had seated her in the front row as she sat there with her little tiny dog which she brought with her.

Later we all met the singer and found out how she heard about the Hollywood Bible study. It turns out that a pizza delivery guy went to her home to deliver a pizza. When the door opened up, the pizza guy noticed it was Natalie Cole. He handed her the pizza and also gave her a flyer to the Hollywood Bible Study. The amazing thing is that Natalie showed up by herself with her little doggy all because of a pizza delivery guy who had the guts to invite her.

Tim Storey was at his best as God used him to bring a message of hope and healing to a whole lot of Hollywood folks. People's lives were genuinely changed for the better, and the impact of the Hollywood Bible Study was felt throughout the entertainment industry and all of Hollywood.

There have only been a handful of Christian ministers who have had such an impact for Christ on Hollywood over many years, and Tim Storey is one of them. His unique style of being real and "down to earth" as we say, draws people from all walks of life, including the movers and shakers of Hollywood. These were awesome years! The cool thing, though, is that the best is yet to come!

"God is not finished with you yet,"

Tim Storey

"I Want You To Do Five Minutes On The Blood."

I traveled with Tim Storey to the state of Washington for a series of services he would be doing at a church where a mutual friend of ours attended. During the day, while we were having lunch, Tim looked straight into my face and said, "Hey Marty, do you want to say a few words tonight?" Never knowing when Tim was serious or if he was joking, I looked right back at him and said, "Anything you need, Tim." He looked at me again and said, "That's not what I asked you." I said again, anything you need!

At this point I knew Tim Storey was up to something; however, I wouldn't find out for about six more hours. When the evening service was about to begin, they seated Tim in the front row on the left side with the senior pastor. They brought me in and seated me on the right side in the front row next to our friend Mike. Everyone began to enter into worship and praise. The next thing I know, Tim Storey gets up from his seat and walks all the way across the front section headed straight for me. With hands lifted and people fully engaged in worship, Tim leans over me and whispers quietly, "I want you to do five minutes on the blood of Christ!" I looked at him with a look of, *Are you serious?*

He looked right in my eyes with a serious look and then proceeded back to his seat. No one in the building knew what he had said to me when he walked over. I thought to myself, *No way, he has to be joking!* I looked over at Tim and he was worshiping God without skipping a beat.

All of a sudden fear gripped me as I said to myself, *"Oh my God, what if he is serious?!"* I sat down while everyone was standing and began the world's fastest bible study trying to come up with five minutes on the blood of Christ. A bead of sweat began to make its way south from my forehead to my chin. The truth is I had about two minutes of material in me which I would have delivered just to not let Tim get me this time.

As I sat there in a cold sweat expecting to go up before hundreds of people without being prepared, Tim Storey was about to be introduced. The music stopped and the Pastor said, "Please welcome Tim Storey!" As everyone cheered for Tim, he got up and made his way to the pulpit. All of a sudden Tim looked at me making eye contact, noticing I was dying a slow death. He then winked at me with a wink of, *"Gotcha!"* I sat there wiping the sweat from my brow saying to myself, *I knew it! I knew it!*

The Flying Cane!

It was a beautiful summer night in Maui, Hawaii. Tim was about to preach in a small on-fire church that night. After the worship ended, Tim began his message, building the people's faith as he always did. I remember his message being so powerful, but then again I've been in hundreds of services over the years where each message was unique and anointed.

There was an elderly man who heard about the services in the newspaper advertising to come and get your healing. That night when Tim began to move in signs and wonders, the man raised his hand and stopped Tim in the middle of his flow. He said, "I've heard that you are a healer and that I could be healed." Without hesitation, Tim Storey told the ushers to bring the older gentleman up to the front. They helped him as he struggled to walk with his cane. Like a wild man of faith, Tim grabbed the man's cane and literally threw it across the church, hitting the wall and making a loud thump.

The people stood watching in shock! Tim took the man's hand and looked him right in the face and said, "Walk with me!" Back and forth Tim helped the man walk, telling him that every step he would take, he would get better. The level of faith began to rise throughout the crowd. All of a sudden the man let go of Tim's hand and started jumping up and down in an excitement I still see in my mind today.

The man was so blessed that two hours after the service had ended and we had been given dinner in the pastor's office, he waited in the parking lot just to say thank you to Tim. As we walked out to our car, the elderly man jumped up from his sitting position and came running over towards us. With tears in his eyes and a grateful heart, he expressed his heartfelt thanks and went on and on saying, "I am healed." Tim told the elderly man that it was *Jesus* who healed him.

As we drove away I said to Tim, "I can't believe you threw that man's cane across the entire church!" Tim said to me, "I can't believe I did that either!"

"Live life by design, not by default."

Tim Storey

"I Can See!"

From 2000 to 2002, I was on staff at a mega church in Southern California. We had 12,000 people attending this great church. We always had the greatest speakers from all over the world, especially Tim Storey. I can honestly say that while I was on staff, no one preacher drew the crowds that Tim drew in.

Being in his hometown, we would see hundreds of people come to the services when Tim would do his Supernatural Miracle Services. One powerful night where God moved in a very special way, people got saved by the droves, and many healings took place.

After the crowd left the sanctuary, there was a lady who was blind sitting in the auditorium who wanted to be prayed for by Tim. Tim came out from the back room where about a dozen friends had gathered around this woman. Tim had her stand up and laid his hand on her head saying, "In the name of Jesus, receive your sight."

The next thing I remember seeing was straight out of the book of Acts. This woman started screaming, "I can see! I can see!" All of us were walking around in shock thinking, O*h my God, her eyes opened up!* Tim asked her to describe his face, and to describe a few articles. She said what she saw and was completely accurate. This woman was healed!

A few days later when I was walking through our church office, the senior pastor's secretary Cindy called me over to share a great report. Cindy told me that the woman had called the church explaining that she had gone to her doctor to get checked out. The doctor was amazed and could not explain what happened! I walked through the office smiling saying, "Thank you Lord. Thank you for healing this woman."

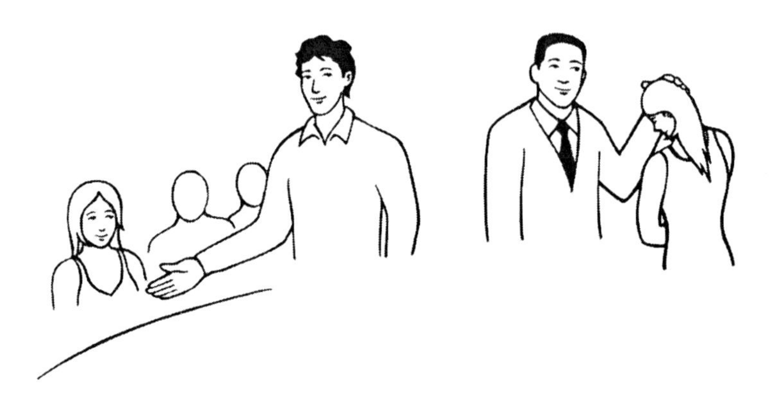

Look At The Girl In The Front, I Think She Likes You!

We were down in Tijuana Mexico where Tim was holding revival services in a church that used to be an old movie theater. People packed the place to standing room only, and they were pressed up to the stage. I was on the stage assisting Tim when he began to pray for people.

The Holy Ghost broke out in the meeting while people were singing, dancing, and praising God. The buzz in the air was energetic and electric! Tim started calling people up on stage to pray for them. The stage soon became packed with people as Tim ran back and forth laying hands on them. I was catching people left and right as the anointing flowed on the stage.

Tim was in the moment and anointing, and so were each of us who were assisting him. The next thing I remember is Tim praying for someone, then turning around and running across the stage. As he was about to pass me, he stopped for a split second and said, "Look at the cute girl in the front. I think she likes you!"

He then continued to the next person without skipping a beat to pray for them. I stood there in a daze, completely taken out of the flow and looking for the cute girl in the front! I am absolutely sure that no one in the building even suspected what Tim had just whispered in my ear. Tim Storey is the only one I know that could move in such a powerful way, and still pull that off! It was really funny as I look back. Tim prayed for all those people and took the time to think about his friend. What a guy!

Hit Him Like Lightning Brah!

This is one of Tim's all time classic stories. I actually was not there for this one, but my experience comes by telling this story for over twenty years. Tim was a young dynamic evangelist preaching in Hawaii at the time. He was beginning to call people up for prayer in his usual style. Tim called up this real skinny white guy to pray for him. There was this big Samoan dude who had just gotten saved earlier in the service that night.

Always the teacher, Tim told the big giant Samoan guy to stand by his side and watch. Tim Storey then told the skinny white guy to close his eyes and raise his hands. As Tim began to pray, he said, "Hit him like lightning! Hit him like lightning!" He was speaking of the Holy Spirit. All of a sudden the huge Samoan punched the skinny white dude in the chest and dropped him like a pancake! Bam! The guy was out cold as he lay there on the floor in front of a startled Tim Storey.

As the crowd gasped, Tim said to the big Samoan, "Hey, why did you do that?" The guy said, "You told me to hit him like lightning, Brah!" Tim said, "Not you man, the Holy Spirit!" Just then Tim jumped on top of the skinny white guy knowing that his future ministry was about to come to an end. Tim yelled, "In the name of Jesus, get up!" The guy stood up to his feet a bit wobbly when Tim asked him the question, "What did that feel like?" The skinny guy said with a big grin, "Wow, that was powerful!"

"Oh My God, How Did You Know My Name?"

Tim can be so funny at times. For years I've gone with him as he has ministered to the mother church of Victory Outreach International. This night Tim was being used in powerful healings and many prophetic words. The climate was awesome and the Holy Spirit was moving upon His people.

Tim called up a girl onto the stage to interview her. As she walked up to Tim Storey, Tim called her by name and said, "Maria, what does it feel like up here on stage?" The girl's eyes opened up really big and she looked like she was in shock! She actually looked like she saw an angel, or perhaps a ghost!

Tim immediately recognized her fear and asked her what was wrong. The girl replied with a shaking voice, "How did you know my name?" Tim looked her right in the eyes and said, "I saw it on your name tag!" She was a greeter.

"Fail forward back into the mercies of God."

Tim Storey

Chapter Four

Lessons Learned Along the Way

Let's Dial In

It's been a privilege and a blessing to be with Tim Storey in hundreds of services over the years. We have literally seen thousands of lives impacted for Christ, healed, delivered, and set free in conferences, churches, and other venues all across America and the world. I have great memories of driving to Tim's house so I could give him a ride to a local meeting.

Because we have known each other for so many years, we naturally would joke around, talk about our funny life experiences, the girls we liked in high school, or any other subject that two life-long friends would talk about.

One night I seemed to be talking Tim's ear off on the way to the church service where about 3,000 people were waiting. I was rambling on and on talking about so much nonsense that I think I was boring myself! Tim couldn't get a word in if he wanted to.

When we got to the service, they introduced Tim Storey as the guest speaker to the applause of the expectant crowd. The people were fired up and ready to hear a word from God. I shall never forget when Tim began speaking; he appeared totally confused and unfocused. I remember sitting there thinking, *What is he saying?* Then the Holy Spirit spoke to me and reminded me of how I was rambling on and on before the service.

The Holy Spirit was teaching me in a moment the importance of being sensitive to the man of God before he was scheduled to speak. It was as though God was showing me the power of influence, and how my actions could positively or negatively affect the people I'm around. After a few minutes of confusion, Tim recomposed himself and went on to preach an awesome message.

From that experience on, every time Tim and I would drive together to a service, we would get about ten minutes away from the church when he would say, "Let's dial in." I would immediately turn off the music, stop talking, and just drive. Tim would begin to review his notes and get mentally prepared to go in and slap the devil up side the head, as he always says.

Whenever Tim and I are driving to a church or conference where he will be preaching; this is the routine that takes place even to this day!

"Marty, Come Up Here and Give That Word."

One of the things I've learned being and working with Tim Storey over the years is to always be alert and ready for anything. I could write a separate book about all of the different things we have seen and experienced in over twenty five years of ministry. In a church in Maui, Hawaii on the second night of services, Tim was preaching strong.

It was a small church that kept the back doors open because of the hot Hawaiian weather. The people had come from all over the island to be a part of this miracle crusade. I somehow found myself standing outside the church talking to someone while Tim was preaching. I allowed myself to become distracted as I recall because I should have been in the church ready to assist Tim at any moment.

The next thing I hear is, "Marty. Where's Marty? Marty come up here and give that word!" When I heard Tim calling my name, I remember looking through the doors from the outside all the way up the aisle seeing Tim search the room for me. The people in the church began looking around searching along with Tim. I immediately ran up the aisle in front of everybody, straight to the preacher. I turned around to face the audience as Reverend Storey stuck the microphone right in front of my face. He said, "Marty, give that word." The crowd of hungry Hawaiians waited patiently to hear a word from God that could potentially change their lives.

Standing there with a blank look on my face, I said to Tim, "I don't have a word!" He looked at me for a split second and said, "Okay, go sit down." The people just stood there puzzled as Tim resumed his message and went on as though nothing had happened. What I learned that night was to stay in the flow or the Spirit and to always be careful of being distracted, especially while doing the work of the Lord. God might want to use us to share a word or a deed that could help somebody else, but it's our responsibility to keep our spiritual ears open.

Let Him Enjoy The Moment!

Several years ago in the state of Maryland, I traveled with Tim to a large church conference. The speakers included Benny Hinn, James Robison, John Avanzini, Pastor Don, and Tim Storey. The church services were packing in about four thousand people a night. I remember standing in the back room before one of the services holding hands in a circle with these great men of God who were asking the Holy Spirit to bless the service. What a privilege for me to be in the company of some world shakers and history makers, as Tim would say.

After the service ended, Pastor Don came over to speak to Tim and me as we were standing in the church foyer. Pastor was so excited about his message and he kept asking Tim, "What did you think of that point I made?" The Pastor continued to share the message he just preached with passion and enthusiasm. Always the encourager and having to add my two cents, with good intentions of course, I was about to speak up when all of a sudden Tim, without breaking eye contact with the Pastor, put his big shoe on top of my shoe, stopping me from saying anything.

Tim Storey knew me so well that he read my body language and sensed I was about to speak while the passionate Pastor was sharing his very special message with us. Later, Tim pulled me aside and taught me a very important lesson that I shall never forget. Tim said to me, "Marty, when the Pastor was sharing his message with us all excited, what were you going to add to what he was saying?" Then Tim said, "Let him have his moment!" I learned that I don't always have to add my opinion when other people are speaking. I should let them have their moment; and who knows? I may learn something!

Holy Ground Before the Battle Ground

I walked in with Tim Storey during the worship time at a church service of a well known minister whose name will remain anonymous. The services were being held in a local hotel at the time. Tim and I were seated in the front row next to the senior pastor. Within minutes, Tim began to sense something different in the Spirit. The worship leader had everyone singing and stomping their feet in a military way.

Now I have been in all types of church services with many different worship styles, but this was different. You got the feeling like the church was filled with young Christians who were being driven to worship in a real aggressive manner. It was as though they needed to get to know Jesus first before becoming warriors! Tim Storey had told me what he was going to preach on before the service. When he took the pulpit, he began talking about walking in love and getting to know Christ first.

Tim changed his whole message on the spot and said that you need to go to the holy ground before the battle ground! The entire atmosphere changed and the anointing fell upon the people that day. I think they got the message! As we drove away from the service, I asked Tim why he changed his sermon. He shared with me how important it is to be sensitive in the Spirit to the people you will be speaking to. He said, "These people need to know Jesus before trying to fight the devil." Wow, I learned another important message that day! After all, Jesus did say, "Apart from me you can do nothing."

Get Them To Trust You First!

I remember when Tim Storey began the successful Hollywood Bible Study back in the mid 1990's. After a season of bible studies in the house of a famous actress named Dyan, we moved the bible studies into a hotel on Sunset Boulevard. Tim began to teach the crowd in a motivational way which was made up of actors, producers, and everyone else in the business.

It's important to note that these industry folks came from various different spiritual backgrounds ranging from Scientology to eastern religions, and everything in between. I remember Tim motivating the people with positive messages; but not too much Bible! I asked Tim why he wasn't sharing the gospel message, and why he was holding back so to speak.

I remember Tim telling me, "Marty, I know what I'm doing!" Then one night on the third or fourth bible study, Tim finished speaking and gave an opportunity for people to receive Jesus Christ as their Lord and Savior. Wow! What a change. He then proceeded to pray for people in his usual Tim Storey style. People began to cry, get saved, and healed right there in a hotel ballroom on the Sunset Strip!

Tim later shared with me that he planned all along to gain the trust of the people first, and that this would take a little time. He told me that at the right time he would go deeper and that the people would be willing to receive God's power after they trusted him more and became open to the Holy Spirit.

I learned a very important lesson about ministering the "Jesus Style" as Tim would say. You can have the greatest message about anything, but the way to get people to hear you begins with establishing a relationship and then getting them to trust you first.

"You can make it."

Tim Storey

Talking In Church

Some of my best memories are the many times sitting next to Tim Storey in a church where he was the guest speaker. Tim would always be teaching me different things about preaching, about the crowd, the environment and so on. As we would sit there during the worship time, Tim would lean over to me and say something interesting that he would observe.

For example, I remember sitting in a church when Tim leaned over to me and said, "Look at the piano player; he is not even flowing with the Spirit." I looked at the piano player and sure enough, he was in a world of his own. He was day dreaming, not even paying attention to the service and the environment. It was amazing to me how Tim would size up the crowd, the environment, the pulse of the atmosphere within minutes.

It was part of being a pro at his craft, knowing and caring about the crowd he was preparing to speak to. He would explain to me how important it was for everyone to be in sync. He would tell me that it's all about the people being touched.

To this day I have never seen anyone pull a crowd back together into the anointing like Tim Storey. He has always been very serious with his ministry to God's people. Every time I get the opportunity to minister to the people of God, I find myself conscious of the environment and the surroundings. Its lessons like these that have helped me to be a more effective minister for Christ. Thanks for the wisdom Dr. Storey.

"Tone It Down A Bit."

While I was on staff at a local church as the executive pastor, Tim was our guest speaker for the night. During praise and worship, Tim sat next to senior Pastor Jim who was my boss, and I sat next to Tim. After the music stopped, I went up to do the announcements. Being an encouragement guy and always trying to look and sound excited; I took the microphone and began to speak. I began to give the announcements with a passion like I was preaching! I might as well have moved right into the offering with the excitement I was causing - so I thought.

I look back now and can remember being a little "over the top" if you know what I mean. After stirring up the crowd after the announcements, I came and sat down next to Tim. He leaned over to me and whispered in my ear, "Tone it down a bit." He later taught me a lesson about not overdoing it during the announcements, and to not take away from the senior pastor's thunder. This became a big lesson for me being a second man several times to different leaders after that. The lesson was to add to the service without drawing the spotlight on me. Tim and his simple wisdom have taught me so much in ministry over the years, and I'm truly grateful.

Power Drives and Napkins

Tim Storey has always been an encourager helping to bring out the best in me. For years Tim and I have taken power drives along the highway, talking faith and speaking life into one another. As busy as Tim can be, he has always taken the time to mentor me and challenge me to become a better person. His wisdom and life experiences have definitely qualified him to speak into many people's lives, including mine.

Our power drives somehow always seem to lead us to some coffee shop, or a Starbucks. It is here where Tim would grab a napkin and begin to draw out a five year timeline of what he planned to do to reach his goals. He would then have me draw out my timeline and encourage me in reaching my goals as well. Little simple things like this are where and how Tim Storey has provided me with nuggets of wisdom over the years. I have learned to cherish and appreciate the many times Tim has poured wisdom, faith, confidence, and hope into me, whether it was flying down the freeway doing 70, or sipping coffee at the local coffee hangout.

"He Looks Like One Of Our Uncles!"

One Sunday Tim and I drove down from the Los Angeles area to a fast growing church in National City, California. Tim was scheduled to speak in three services back to back at Cornerstone Church of San Diego; a great church I might add. Our good friend Pastor Sergio and his team have always taken care of us while ministering there.

As usual, the drive from north to south was full of great conversation between Tim and me; full of funny stories and inspiring challenges. As we approached the church parking lot, one of the ushers from the church saw us from a distance and came running as fast as he could to move a few parking cones for us. The usher was a Hispanic gentleman, probably in his late fifties. With the biggest smile on his face, this humble man reminded Tim and me in an instant what real servant-hood was all about.

As we drove past the nice guy to park the car, Tim said, "He looks like one of our uncles!" We sat in the car for a brief moment as Tim said, "Hey Marty, you see that older gentleman? If this whole trip was to come down to minister just to that one man, it would all be worth it." Then he said, "Let's never forget where we came from, huh?" The wonderful usher caught up to us and offered to help us with anything we needed.

To some this little story might seem petty, but the fact that this story is being written a few years later is proof that this one man influenced our lives! I don't remember his name, and I'm sure Tim doesn't either, but what we did learn is that being a servant sometimes comes disguised as a person looking like one of our uncles!

Prayer Changes Things!

Back in the late 1980's when Tim Storey hosted his first national conference; I remember watching Tim go to God in prayer for a special request. Tim was a young dreamer who had stepped out in faith to host what turned out to be one of the most successful national conferences that year.

Three days into this huge gathering where thousands of people from all around the world assembled, the financial budget for the event was around eighty thousand dollars short. Tim was carrying a huge burden of responsibility on his shoulders to lead this rather large undertaking.

I remember one night as many of us who helped with the ministry all shared a big house together with Tim and his family. From the living room area as I walked towards my room, I heard a sound coming from the room where Tim was staying. His door was slightly cracked as I could see him on his knees calling out to God. I remember watching him for a moment thinking to myself, God please hear his prayer.

Tim was and has always been a firm believer that prayer changes things. Actually he knew that it was God who could change things through prayer. Well by the end of the conference, the Lord did a financial miracle causing the conference to meet budget and then some. What I learned from Tim was that our God answers prayers when our hearts are in the right place.

"Never give up."

Tim Storey

Chapter Five

Tough Times!

"You're a champion."

Tim Storey

Randy

One of my best friends was Randy Storey, Tim's older brother. Randy went on to be with the Lord a few years back. He is in Heaven now. Growing up with the Storey family has been such a blessing to me. Bessie Storey, Tim's mom, is like my second mother, and Berna and Paige, Tim's sisters, are like sisters to me. Randy was a few years older then Tim and me. He was one very special person, and he always made me laugh.

Tim had lost his father while he was a young boy and a sister a few years later. Losing his big brother was very hard for Tim as you can imagine. Randy loved the Lord but fought certain battles in his life. Over the years, Tim would call me while he was somewhere in the U.S preaching, and ask me to go check on his brother Randy who would encounter a setback or end up in some kind of situation.

I knew that Tim loved his brother very much, and he was always concerned for him, as was the whole family. Randy had been doing so well when, unfortunately, he ended up having a setback in his life. One day Tim called and asked me to go visit Randy who was staying at his house.

Randy was really going through a tough time and I tried to encourage him that things would get better. I remember getting frustrated with Randy because it was hard seeing him that way. When it came time for me to leave, Randy followed me to my car. As I opened my car door and got in, he leaned in the window and said to me, "Marty, you know I love you." As I drove away, these would be the last words I would ever hear Randy say.

When I received the phone call that Randy had passed, I rushed over to Bessie Storey's home where the family had gathered. I went straight to Bessie with a big hug and just held her, and then grabbed Tim in my arms and just hugged him tight. We cried together at a time that was very difficult. It turned out to be one of the hardest times for the Storey family, and certainly one of the toughest times for my friend, Tim.

Tim loved Randy with the love of a true brother, and has always honored his life and memory. This was a tough time of pain for Tim and the Storey family, but we all know that Randy is triumphant and in Heaven now. We will see you soon Brother Randy.

"Remember, to grow is to change, however

painful it may be at the time."

Tim Storey

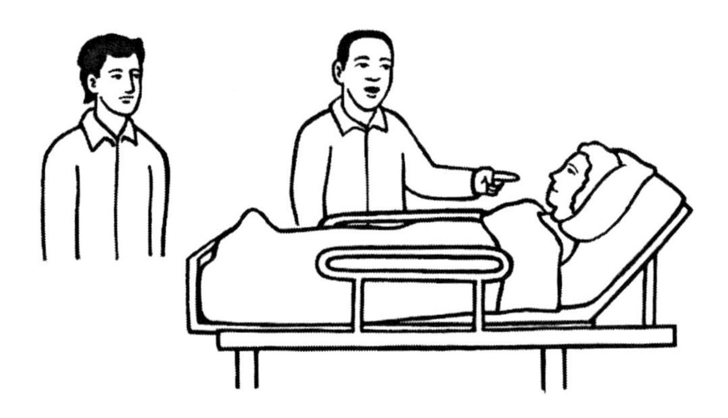

"You Will Live."

One of the reasons I love Tim Storey so much is because he has always been there for my family. A few years back, I flew into the Los Angeles airport, returning from a trip to Europe. I went from there to visit my mother, Genevieve, who happens to be like a second mother to Tim, and immediately noticed she was in pain.

Within a few hours we had her in the hospital going through several tests. The doctors quickly determined and told our family that my mother was dying of cancer and had less than six months to live. Needless to say our family was devastated. I called my friend Tim who was preaching somewhere across the United States. Without hesitation, Tim caught a plane for L.A. and made it to the hospital within one day.

I will never forget when Tim entered the room to come and pray for my mom. My mother lit up like a candle when she saw Tim because she knew that God used him in signs and wonders. Her faith shot up and the atmosphere in the room literally changed! Tim began to read some healing scriptures to my mother and began to lay hands on her and pray for her. With our immediate family in the room at the time, Tim began to prophesy over my mother. He looked right at her and said, "You will not die. You will live." It was so powerful, and you could cut the anointing in the room with a knife! He went on to say that our family needed my mother and that it wasn't her time yet. She had already been given a death sentence by the doctors before Tim Storey prophesied.

One week later we took my mom home from the hospital. I will forever be grateful to my friend Tim Storey for flying across the country to stand by my mother's bedside in her time of need. When I think of Tim Storey, I think of a great man of faith, an awesome evangelist, a dynamic speaker and communicator, but most of all, a true friend to my dear mother and family. Tim, you're the best!

"You can make it."

Tim Storey

Chapter Six

The Current Years

"Eric, Write That Check For...? "

A few years back, I was honored and privileged to work for the Full Gospel Businessmen Fellowship International. Tim had introduced me to his friend Richard Shakarian, the International President of the largest Christian laymen organization in the world. I was blessed to become the Director of USA Chapters, working with the inner circle of the president.

We hosted a World Convention in a major U.S. city where Tim was scheduled to speak the last night of the convention. Tim has always been a favorite guest convention speaker over the years. Historically, this organization has obtained the greatest Christian leaders as convention speakers from Billy Graham to Oral Roberts, Chuck Smith to Kathryn Kuhlman, Benny Hinn to R.W. Schambach, just to name a few. Almost every major Christian leader since the 1950s, along with politicians and great business leaders have spoken at World Conventions for FGBMFI.

As we approached the last night of the convention where about 5,000 people from over 80 nations were attending, the finances were not meeting the convention budget. Tim Storey's financial advisor, who happens to be my brother Eric Celaya, was sitting in the front row. As long as I've known Tim, he has always been an incredible giver.

After speaking a powerful message as he always did, Tim began to speak regarding the offering. Instead of being ready to accept his well-deserved offering from the fellowship, Tim told the crowd that he would not be taking any money, but that he wanted to sow into the convention and the Full Gospel Businessmen. Not only did he tell the crowd that he would not be taking any money, he said to the crowd "Eric Celaya - everyone this is my financial advisor - write a check for three thousand dollars and put it in the offering."

All of a sudden, a financial miracle took place! Because of what Tim Storey did, the people began to spontaneously get out of their seats bringing money to the front stage. It was amazing to see how one man's generosity could spark such an overwhelming overflow of giving. Because I was one of the staff who counted all of the convention revenues along with the ministry treasure, I can honestly say that we more than met the budget that night! This was just one of many times I witnessed the generosity of Tim Storey over the years.

Falling Out Everywhere!

Another fun memory for me was at another Full Gospel World Convention. We were honored to have one of the right hand Archbishops to Pope John Paul the second as a special guest. He was at the convention representing the Catholic Hierarchy binging well wishes from the Pope himself.

This was very special. I remember every night when the Archbishop was introduced; he would say a few words and wave to the crowd with his traditional sign of the cross. He was always introduced as "Your Excellency" from the international president of Full Gospel. I think you know what I mean. The night Tim Storey spoke at the convention with all of the Full Gospel leaders, dignitaries, and of course the Archbishop sitting on the platform, Tim preached a message of power and faith.

I remember it being a charged atmosphere of the Holy Ghost that engulfed everyone in the building. Tim began to call out the leaders from their seats so he could pray and lay hands on them. One by one I watched successful businessmen from all around the world, leaders, dignitaries, and everyone Tim Storey laid hands on fall out under the power of the Holy Spirit. What I remember and shall never forget is the Archbishop from Rome sitting in his chair wearing his traditional outfit with a look like, "What is happing here?!"

He seemed to be enjoying the power of God being displayed; however, one would get the feeling that this was not the normal environment for him! As the leaders would fall out, I watched the Archbishop attempt to bless them with the sign of the cross as they either flew by him like a high speed train, or hit the floor in front of him with a thump. It was hilarious! The night ended with so many people being touched and blessed.

After it was over, the look on the face of the Archbishop seemed to say, "This was cool." What I appreciate about Tim Storey is that he always is himself and allows God's gifts to flow no matter who is in the crowd. It was awesome; but I have to tell you, it was very funny!

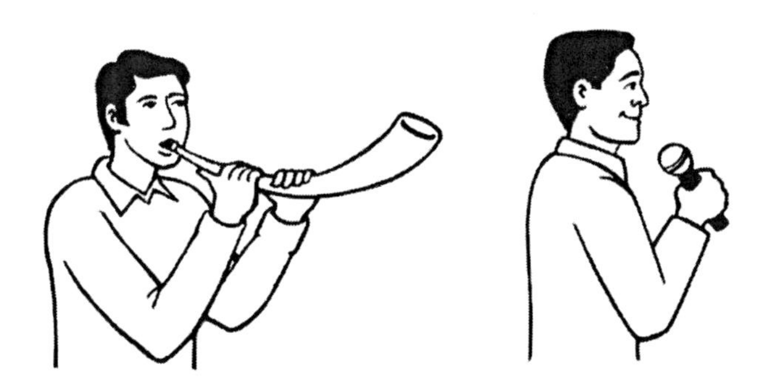

The Shofar!

One more short story that took place at a Full Gospel Businessmen World convention cracks me up. We were all celebrating the "Year of Jubilee," and the leaders would open up every meeting with the blowing of the Shofar. This is a ram's horn that sounds like a trumpet. After a while, when the International President introduced Tim Storey as the main speaker, Tim took the microphone and began to calmly speak to the crowd.

I was sitting in the front row watching Tim speak, and the President of FGBMFI, Richard S., was standing on the platform about ten feet behind Tim. Next to Richard lay the shofar on a table that was just begging for someone to pick it up and let it rip! I was watching Tim speak softly with one eye, and I had my other eye on Richard who was staring at the shofar. Just as I got the sense that Richard was going to pick up the shofar, he did.

Imagine Tim Storey speaking and greeting the crowd of thousands when all of a sudden, for no reason, Richard picks up the horn and blows it towards the crowd behind Tim with all of his might. Tim jumped about three feet forward from the blast as he was startled by the shofar. It was so unbelievably funny; I almost got a side ache. Tim looked at Richard wondering, *What was that?!* Richard casually placed the shofar on the table as if nothing happened. Tim just resumed his speaking while the whole crowd smiled scratching their heads saying, "What just happened?" You had to be there on this one.

"Oh No, You Can't Come Into the Room Tim!"

Tim Storey has always been good at talking his way into any place. I was in the delivery room coaching Elisabeth while she was giving birth to our first born, baby Sara. Sara's little head was just starting to pop out into the world when all of a sudden the nurse came up to me and said, "There is some man and woman wanting to come in here."

Just then the door started to open and I saw Tim stick his big head in with a great big smile! (Can you see Tim Now?) I ran to the door and pushed him back outside saying, "You can't come in here! What are you doing?!"

Tim and Cindy were standing outside the room laughing it up, while Elisabeth was in the room pushing away! I said, "How did you get up here? Go away!" Elisabeth delivered our beautiful daughter that day, or shall I say that hour, and she has grown up knowing this hospital intruder as Uncle Tim.

"Tim, She's One Year Old!"

One of the things I love about Tim Storey is that he is always aware and conscious of his surroundings. When it comes to church services, events, conferences, and any other gatherings where Tim is present, he always makes sure that it's upbeat and exciting!

Our daughter Sara was celebrating her first birthday party at our home, complete with food, a piñata, pin the tail on the donkey, the birthday cake, and all of her cousins and friends. Little Chloe and Isaiah Storey were running around having fun with Sara and all the children. After we did the birthday cake, opened the presents, and all of the normal birthday party festivities you would experience at a child's party, we adults went into my living room to relax with some coffee.

I'll never forget Tim sitting next to me getting a bit fidgety. I was sipping my coffee when all of a sudden Tim leaned over to me with a serious face and said, "Hey Marty, we have to get this party moving!" I looked at Tim and said, "She's one year old; it's her birthday party. Relax!" Tim snapped out of it and said, "Oh." Then he took a sip of his coffee.

This Man Has Been Praising God For 10 Hours!

This story is a personal favorite of mine. I will do my best to communicate this funny Tim Storey moment. I'm sitting in the second row surrounded by pastors who were all attending this conference in West Covina, California. Tim was running around praying for people as the power of God hit the place. The excitement and anointing was heavy in the church! People were standing in the front section waiting for Tim to lay hands on them.

After Tim would pray for people, they would all walk back to their seats on their own. One guy who Tim prayed for kept standing in the front with his hands raised up. He must have been standing there for at least twenty minutes all by himself with his hands lifted and his eyes closed. Tim would run right past this man several times who continued to stand there enjoying his time with God.

All of a sudden Tim came running around the corner. While praying for people, he stopped in front of the worshipping man for no apparent reason. He pointed to the man and said to the crowd in a funny voice, "Now this man's been praising God for ten hours!" After saying that, he took off running again leaving the man standing there in shock.

Tim continued to pray for people with out skipping a beat! What I remember are fifteen or more pastors cracking up asking each other, "What was that?" It was so funny because none of us knew what he meant! I later let Tim know how funny it was when he said that to the poor guy who was worshipping so intently. I said, "Hey Tim, why did you do that to that guy?" He said back to me, "Do what?"

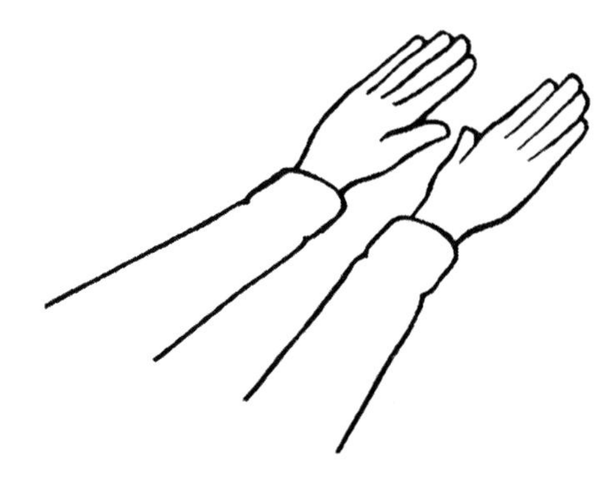

"Everybody Stretch Forth Your Hands!"

This is another hilarious Tim Storey classic that I must share with you. As you will see, you can imagine that I begged Tim to let me tell this one. Tim was praying for people in a church in Texas one night. Keep in mind that he has prayed for literally tens of thousands of people over many years. The ushers would bring people up to be prayed for from each side of the stage.

Tim finished praying for one man and turned around to see who was coming up next. Just then a beautiful tall woman came walking up with her big hair and her Texas walk. Just picture this with me. Tim put the microphone up to her and asked her what was wrong. Just then the woman in her Texas accent said, "I have a lump on my breast." Without hesitation Tim looked at the crowd and said, "Everybody please stretch forth your hands and pray for this woman because she has large breasts!" The church erupted in laughter as Tim stood there in a daze and said, "Did I just say that? Did I just say what I think I said?" This would go down as one of the funniest slip ups in church history!

The whole crowd of people laughed hysterically for several minutes watching Tim die a thousand deaths! Only Tim Storey could eventually talk his way out of that one! This one still makes us laugh to this day.

Gag Gifts!

A long-time tradition between Tim and me are the gag gifts we give each other on our birthdays. Well if I am completely honest, it's more like the gag gifts I give him. Over the years I have given Tim the craziest, stupidest gifts you can imagine. As I write this, on his last birthday he opened up a present only to find two of my preaching CDs; needless to say he was not shocked.

The best all-time gift was a few years ago. I took Tim's best selling book, "Utmost Living," and had my face transposed on the book cover. I changed the name to Marty Celaya all over the book, and rewrote the endorsements from all of the famous people on the back of the cover thanking me for helping their lives.

I was sitting with Tim's family and a few friends at a nice restaurant when Tim began to open his gifts. As he unwrapped my gift, which appeared to be a book, he pulled out a copy of Utmost Living, and seeing my face on the cover he almost fell out of his chair.

Tim laughed so hard that we almost had to resuscitate him! He read the endorsements on the back that gave praise and glory to me with tears in his eyes. It was such a funny moment to see Tim Storey bust up like never before. My only problem is thinking how I'm going to top this all-time best gag gift. Perhaps I will star in one of Tim Storey's TV performances - as him!

Christmas Eve Shopping

I have learned to cherish the times I spend with Tim. Weather it's driving around in the convertible feeling good on purpose, sitting in a coffee shop talking vision and strategy, being at a family function, ministering together on the road, or just hanging out, spending time with my friend of many years.

Because we are both busy people living busy lives, one of our traditions over the years has been our last minute Christmas shopping spree on Christmas Eve. Like two men on a mission, Tim and I would hit the Brea Mall gathering those last minute gift items for our friends and families. It's amazing how much shopping we can get done when we truly focus! We would catch up after being so busy in our businesses and ministries. It's simple memories like these that cause me to appreciate my friendship with Tim Storey.

"Pull Over, This is The Police!"

Not long ago Tim and I drove down to a great church in the San Diego area where Tim was scheduled to preach multiple services. I picked him up in my Mercedes and we hit the 5 Freeway south, enjoying the ride. I was driving a bit fast in the fast lane when suddenly lights started flashing in my rear-view mirror.

We were pulled over by this young, rookie, Highway Patrolman. He came up to the window and asked me if I knew why he pulled me over. I told him I was in a hurry to get this minister to the church where he was supposed to speak. I then shifted into beg mode and began to plead for a break from Mr. Highway Patrol!

I told him that in my business, I help a lot of law enforcement officers with their financial planning; he was not moved. He stood there and began to write a ticket when all of a sudden Tim Storey decided to give it a shot. Tim said, "Sir, I am a minister scheduled to speak at a big church in a few hours. My friend is just trying to get me there on time. Please don't give him a ticket."

Again the stone faced young officer was not persuaded, so now Tim kicked into beg mode! I sat there smiling bowing my head as Tim began to drop names. "I am a life coach to the Hollywood Stars," Tim told the guy. "I am affiliated with Oprah Winfrey's people!" The policeman continued to write the ticket, then handed it to me and said, "You guys slow down." Tim and I drove away cracking up saying to one another, "I guess we don't have it anymore!" It was funny. Oh, by the way, Tim paid for the ticket.

Marty, I Have Some Suits For You!

I've got to tell you, Tim Storey is such a giver. Because of Tim's lifestyle and profession, he has always worn the nicest suits you can imagine. Suits like Hugo Boss, Armani, Prada, and Canali just to name a few. For several years Tim, in his generosity, would call me and say something like this, "Hey Marty, I have some suits for you!"

Whenever I would get that call, it was like Christmas; I'm not teasing. Tim would give me three, four, or sometimes seven jackets at a time. The amazing thing is the coats have always fallen on me, fitting perfectly. Because Tim is just a little shorter than I am, I normally would have to get the cuffs in the pants fixed. This has never been a problem.

These suits and jackets have been such a blessing to me from Tim over many years, and they keep on coming. As I am writing this story here in 2010, just a few days ago I received the Christmas call! This time Tim overwhelmed me with about eight top-of-the-line suits that are sure to bring out the dapper in me! He has given me so many suits over the years, and I have in turn blessed others with many of them also.

I said to Tim as he was giving them to me, "Tim, I don't know what to say. This is too much!" He smiled at me and said, "Just try on the coats. It's nothing; we're brothers!" This is the type of guy he is. Thanks Tim.

"Tonight we're going to slap the devil up side the head."

Tim Storey

The Usual!

This is another Tim Storey classic that just needs to be told. I was not with Tim several years ago when this occurrence took place; however, Tim has used this story as an illustration many times over the years. Just this morning, the morning as I am writing this, I went with Tim to a church where he was going to speak. On the way, we stopped at the local donut shop to pick up a cup of coffee and a croissant.

It was early in the morning and the local regulars were already there, sipping their brew and sharing their stories with one another. As we walked out, Tim said to me, "Marty, do you remember the story of 'The Usual'?" I said to Tim, "Of course I remember that story." It happened like this.

When Tim was younger, he used to frequent a local donut shop in his city. One day as he walked in to get a donut and some coffee, he heard the lady behind the counter say, "Hi Ralph, would you like the usual?" Ralph responded, "The usual." As Tim stood in line, the lady said to the next guy, "Hi John, the usual?"

John said, "The usual." Every time Tim would go to this donut shop, he would hear the lady ask all of the regulars if they wanted the usual.

Tim later learned an awesome lesson from the donut shop experience which he has shared with thousands of people all across the world. He talks about how so many people settle for "the usual" in life when God wants so much more for them. He encourages people everywhere how an "Utmost God" wants "Utmost Children!" This classic story is a constant reminder of not settling for anything less then God's best for our lives; therefore I'd like to end this short story by asking you this question, "May I take your order?"

"Come on somebody."

Tim Storey

Thank You, Tim Storey, For Being There For Our Family!

The Bible is very clear that we will go through many different seasons in life. In the book of Ecclesiastes, chapter three, it says there is a time for everything and a season for every activity under the sun. It begins by saying there is a time to be born, and a time to die. It goes on to talk about the different times in life. My family and I are so grateful to Tim Storey for being here in our time of need. Our beloved mother, who is eighty two years old, is preparing to go to Heaven due to illness in her life. Just yesterday my friend Tim came to our home to pray with my sisters, my brother, my dad, my nephew, his girlfriend, and our mom.

Tim sat by our mother's bedside and shared about the palm tree as written in Psalm 92. He described our mother as being a special lady who has endured so much in life, like the bending of a palm tree. I will never forget how he told our mom that as a palm tree bends, it does not break. He told her how resilient she has been over so many years.

Tim then shared about the second important parallel of the palm tree. He said that the roots of the tree go really deep! He then encouraged our mother of how her roots have gone so far, touching so many lives, from her children to her great grandchildren. He continued to assure our mom that her beautiful spirit will live on in all of us. Tim said that the palm tree also provides shade to everything it covers.

He encouraged us so much before leading us in a special prayer over mom. The anointing was so powerful, and you could feel the presence of the Holy Spirit in the room. Through tears, we all shared a special moment together which I shall never forget. Mom then hugged Tim and said, "I have always considered you as my adopted son!" Tim then smiled with that big grin of his. We all chuckled when I said, "Wait, you mean we are real brothers?" Thanks Tim. You are loved. Mom went home to be with Jesus on May23, 2010.

Chapter Seven

The Future Looks Bright; The Value of True Friendship

I hope you have enjoyed just some of the special moments I've shared with my best friend, Tim. These awesome experiences reflect a life-long journey spanning over 30 years of great times; however, let it be known, there will be many more to come. For this reason I want to say, "The future looks bright!"

From an early age, Tim has been and continues to be one of God's special ambassadors. A young man with a dream in his heart to touch the world for Christ has indeed become a reality. It has been a privilege for me to grow up with him and his wonderful family all these years.

Special honor and credit should be mentioned to Tim's mother Bessie who has been an anchor in the faith for her family and many friends. Bessie is like my second mom, by the way. Tim's sisters, Berna and Paige have been dear friends and co-ministers, helping me to become a better person along the way. My children have grown up with Tim's children over the years. Our children are beautiful young people with great parents. (I had to throw that in.)

I have titled this chapter, "The Future Looks Bright; The Value of True Friendship," because to have a friend like Tim for all these years has not only been unique, it's been priceless. He has taught many of us over several years about the value of being a good friend first, and then attracting great people into our lives.

One of his awesome messages over the years is found in the book of Ecclesiastes, chapter four. The scripture says: *Two are better than one, because they have a good return for their work: If one falls down, his friend can help him up. But pity the man who falls and has no one to help him up! Also, if two lie down together, they will keep warm. But how can one keep warm alone? Though one may be overpowered, two can defend themselves. A cord of three strands is not quickly broken.* (NIV version)

Tim has been a wonderful example of how the Bible says, "Two are better than one." He has included so many people into his life and purpose allowing others to prosper, including myself. His lifestyle has and continues to exemplify this portion of scripture which describes what a true friend really is and does.

Along with teaching us to be good friends first, Tim has preached for many years about how "Like attracts like." I shall never forget his illustration of the man who came walking out of the department store, walking like a duck! Tim proceeded to say that right behind this duck-walking-man came his wife who walked like a duck also. Then the three children, one by one, strutted out from the store; Bam! Three more ducks!

His point to be made followed the old saying, "The apple doesn't fall far from the tree." But Tim in his illustrative way has taught us that if we act like a duck, we're probably going to attract a whole lot of the same into our lives.

When we talk about the word "value" we can actually go in many directions. In regards to true friendship, though, my first thought is the word "priceless." Life is really about relationships, beginning with the friendship our Heavenly Father has with us.

The Bible describes in Proverbs 18:24 that *"there is a friend who sticks closer than a brother."* Jesus himself shows us through the scripture how priceless His true friendship is with us, and how important it is for us to be a real friend to our brothers and sisters.

One of Tim's classic messages from way back in the day was titled, "Walking in Love." Tim taught us how everything in life was meaningless if we didn't do it in a spirit of love. Jesus said in John's Gospel, chapter 15, *"My command is this: Love each other as I have loved you. Greater love has no one than this; that he lay down his life for his friends. You are my friends, if you do what I command."*

Tim has consistently taught thousands of people over many years about the value of being a good friend. I have been blessed to have him as a true friend who has always added value to my life.

As I conclude this book of short stories and awesome life experiences I have shared with Tim over half of my life, let me say again that there are many great stories that are yet to be written. The future really does look bright!

To you the reader, I hope you caught a deeper insight of the many wonderful sides that make up Tim Storey. From the young, energetic, funny guy, to the inspirational dreamer, to the man of godly wisdom, and to the dynamic influencer he is today.

My hope is that you cherish the special people that God has placed in your life. It is also my wish that you be encouraged to write your own life's story developing wonderful moments with those you love and care about.

Thank you buddy for everything you've ever done for me and my family, and for all of the great days that lie ahead. Thank you, Lord Jesus, for my best friend, Tim.

SPECIAL ACKNOWLEGMENTS

I would like to take a few moments to acknowledge some special people who have positively influenced me and have helped me write this book. First, I sincerely thank you, Tim Storey, for being a true friend to me and for always being there for our family.

I would also like to thank all of the Storey family including Bessie, Berna, Paige, and Randy whom we miss so much. All of you and your extended family have and continue to be an inspiration to people everywhere. Thank you Chloe and Isaiah for letting uncle Marty spend so much time with your daddy when he should have been taking you to Chuck-E-Cheese more often. Just joking!

I want to thank my family for always standing with me to help shape me and make me into a better person. Thanks to my wonderful parents, Otto and Genevieve Celaya for all of your love and support in my life. Thank you to my sisters, Lydia and Lisa for helping to raise me from day one! Special thanks are for my mentor and brother Eric Celaya who has poured a lifetime of wisdom, love, and support into me.

Thank you Elisabeth for allowing me to support Tim and his ministry over so many years as I felt called to do; I know it took a lot of time. Sara and Adam, not only do I dedicate this book to you, but I thank you for being such wonderful children making me so proud to be your dad.

My family thanks would not be complete without mentioning all of my nieces and nephews, cousins, uncles and aunts, and basically all of our extended family and friends who number in the hundreds. I would like to thank many of the spiritual leaders who may or may not have been mentioned in this book.

I would like to thank Pastor Ron Prinzing for being my first spiritual father, teaching me the foundations of the faith. Also, thank you to the ministers who gave me opportunities to use my gifts and talents. Thank you Richard Shakarian for giving me my first full time ministry position with FGBMFI. Thank you Pastor's Jim Reeve, Bob Reeve, and Jim Willoughby for allowing me to serve and learn in ministry positions at your great churches.

The truth is, there are far too many other men and women who have helped along the way; too many to count. At last I want to thank those who helped make this book a reality.

Thank you Jill Voorhees Kiefer and Sylvia Celaya for making sure our words were spelled right. Special thanks to my nephew Kartal Alyuz who heads up Parable Media Entertainment for our cover pictures and book construction. Thanks Scott Docherty for our cover design. Thank you Mr. Jeremy Wray for your awesome skills as an artist. Not only are you a world class skateboarder, but your art pictures rock!

Last but not least, I thank you Lord Jesus Christ for giving me a wonderful life with so many beautiful people in it. I am so thankful for the many experiences I have enjoyed, and for my life that is yet to be lived.

Marty Celaya

CONTACT INFORMATION:

For more information concerning all of Tim Storey's books, products, motivational materials, speaking engagements, and ministry tools, please contact:

Storey Dreams Foundation
P: 562.590.7900
F: 562.590.6312
info@storeystyle.com

To contact Marty Celaya for speaking engagements, leadership workshops, and "My Best Friend Tim" books, please contact:

www.encouragementintl.org
Email: Martycelaya@yahoo.com

Marty Celaya is a Christian Businessman and Minister residing in Southern California who truly believes that the most important things in life are the relationships we establish along life's journey. Next to his personal relationship with our Lord and Savior Jesus Christ, Marty is grateful for his family, his beautiful children, and his wonderful friendships with people all around the world. Known as an encourager, a networker, and a connector of people, Marty Celaya's mission is to help other people's visions come to pass.

Breinigsville, PA USA
09 March 2011
257264BV00003B/2/P

9 781613 790113